"I have a pro[posal]

His hands slid under the lapels of her jacket, pushing them apart, while the gray eyes made a slow, lingering survey of the swell of her rounded breasts under the clinging camisole.

Chay said softly, "You've grown up beautifully, Adie."

"Don't call me that. And don't handle me, either," Adrien added, her voice quivering. "You bought a house. I was not included in the price."

"It occurs to me that this house lacks something. It needs a mistress," he said softly. "And so do I. And you, my sweet Adrien, are the perfect candidate."

RED HOT REVENGE

There are times in a man's life...
when only seduction will settle old scores!

Pick up our exciting series of revenge-based
romances—they're red-hot,
so get ready to be singed!

The Marriage Debt
by
Daphne Clair
On Sale in September #2347

Sara Craven

MISTRESS ON LOAN

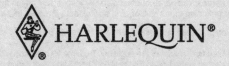

HARLEQUIN®

TORONTO • NEW YORK • LONDON
AMSTERDAM • PARIS • SYDNEY • HAMBURG
STOCKHOLM • ATHENS • TOKYO • MILAN • MADRID
PRAGUE • WARSAW • BUDAPEST • AUCKLAND

ISBN 0-373-12338-8

MISTRESS ON LOAN

First North American Publication 2003.

Copyright © 2000 by Sara Craven.

All rights reserved. Except for use in any review, the reproduction or
utilization of this work in whole or in part in any form by any electronic,
mechanical or other means, now known or hereafter invented, including
xerography, photocopying and recording, or in any information storage
or retrieval system, is forbidden without the written permission of the
publisher, Harlequin Enterprises Limited, 225 Duncan Mill Road,
Don Mills, Ontario, Canada M3B 3K9.

All characters in this book have no existence outside the imagination of
the author and have no relation whatsoever to anyone bearing the same
name or names. They are not even distantly inspired by any individual
known or unknown to the author, and all incidents are pure invention.

This edition published by arrangement with Harlequin Books S.A.

® and TM are trademarks of the publisher. Trademarks indicated with
® are registered in the United States Patent and Trademark Office, the
Canadian Trade Marks Office and in other countries.

Visit us at www.eHarlequin.com

Printed in U.S.A.

CHAPTER ONE

IT WAS the time of day that Adrien loved best—those quiet, early-morning hours when she had the house completely to herself. Before the painters arrived, and the joiners and plasterers, and work began again to restore Wildhurst Grange to its former glory.

She liked to move slowly from room to room, opening shutters and flinging back the drapes from the newly curtained windows to admit the pale late-summer sun. Letting herself move forward in her imagination to the time when she and Piers would be married, and living here, and she would no longer be simply the interior designer but the mistress of the house. And Piers's wife.

That was the best part of all, and the thought always made her slightly breathless—as if she could hardly believe her own luck, the way her life had fallen so sweetly into place.

Because there was a wonderful symmetry about it all. About the way they'd met at Wildhurst all those years before, when he'd come to her rescue when she was in trouble, and then how the house had brought them back together, when Piers had inherited the neglected property from his late uncle, Angus Stretton, and needed a designer to help plan the restoration.

And soon, she thought, it would be finished, and theirs to share as man and wife. Bringing the chain of events full circle.

Her only regret was that Piers wasn't there to watch the regeneration of his future home, but was working in Portugal.

'I'm sorry too, my darling,' he'd murmured as he held her on their last evening together. 'But it has to be done. Quite apart from all the work it needs, the Grange won't be a cheap proposition to run, and I have to make sure the money's there, that we don't have to scrimp and make do with second best. I want you to have everything.'

'But I don't need everything,' Adrien had protested, slightly troubled. 'And we could start slowly—just doing up the rooms we're going to use.'

But Piers wouldn't hear of that. He wanted the whole house finished—'so that we're not living with workmen and out of boxes for the next ten years, my sweet.'

He had a point, Adrien supposed, with a sigh. And she wrote to him every week, sending a concise progress report, including colour charts and fabric samples, while he telephoned and sent e-mails and faxes.

But it wasn't the same as having him there.

'Once the company's established, I won't leave you again, I promise,' he'd whispered. 'And just think what a marvellous showcase the Grange will make for your talents,' he'd added cajolingly. 'Business will boom when we start entertaining.'

Adrien had laughed and hugged him, but inwardly she was determined that the Grange would be first and foremost their home—their private sanctuary.

In any case, she wasn't sure she could cope with a boom, she thought wryly. Before she'd met Piers again, and fallen in love, and become involved with the restoration project, her business had already been thriving.

It was basically a two-woman operation—herself, as designer, and Zelda March, who was a local girl and a brilliant seamstress. A to Z Design hadn't lacked for work since it had opened its doors.

Although it certainly wasn't what she'd had in mind when she'd completed her training, she admitted. Coming back to the quiet country town where she'd been brought up hadn't been part of the plan at all. But her mother's sudden death three years ago had caused her to rethink her future completely.

Adrien, rushing down from London, had had to face the fact that she was now alone in the world. But she'd also inherited Listow Cottage, and some money from her mother's life insurance, which had given her a measure of independence for the first time.

Her life, she had realised bleakly, could change. But she hadn't seen how until she'd run into Zelda at the funeral.

It had been a long time since they'd seen each other. They'd been in the same year at school, but not on the same track. Zelda had been the local wild child, always in trouble with the authorities for smoking, under-age drinking and hanging round with boys. In her final year she'd amazed everyone by winning the Home Economics prize with a baby's wooden cradle, which she'd trimmed with handmade curtains and a beautiful embroidered quilt, as well as making a complete set of baby clothes.

Before she was seventeen she was pregnant by a local garage mechanic, and their hasty marriage had been followed by an even speedier divorce.

Adrien had been surprised to see her in the congregation at the church, and, on impulse, had invited her back to the cottage.

'I thought the world of your mum,' Zelda confided, when the other mourners had departed. She looked sadly round the sitting room. 'It was only a couple of months ago that I made these loose covers and curtains for her.'

On the surface, Zelda didn't seem to have changed much. The dark spiky hair was still much in evidence, and so was the nose stud. But as they talked Adrien sensed a new, quiet maturity about her. A strength to the set of her thin shoulders that impressed Adrien. And the workmanship on the soft furnishings was superb.

'Do you work freelance?' Adrien questioned.

Zelda shook her head. 'I wish. I do customer orders for Beasley and Co in Enderton, but the pay's rock-bottom. I've tried doing some work at home, but I'm back living with Mum and Dad and the kids, and there just isn't room. Not with Smudge too.'

'Smudge?'

'That's what I call my son. His real name's Kevin, like his father, but I don't want to be reminded.'

'I suppose not.' Adrien bit her lip. 'It seems a shame that you can't work for yourself. You're really good.'

'There's no chance of that.' Zelda shrugged. 'Dad goes mad when the sewing machine comes out. And he's not too thrilled to have Smudge around anyway, so I try not to rock the boat.'

It was only a brief exchange, but it stuck in Adrien's mind.

During the days that followed, she set about working out a business plan. There was undoubtedly a gap in the market. Beasley's were no real competition, and there was no one else within miles who could offer a complete interior design service. She could pinpoint all the genuine craftsmen in the area to use as sub-contractors, and with Zelda to cover the soft furnishing side…

Premises might be a problem, she realised. Until she took a good look at the cottage. It wasn't large, and it needed modernisation, but around its rear courtyard there were old stables and outbuildings, unused for years and ripe for conversion. There was space for workrooms, an office, and a self-contained flat.

'Are you serious about this?' Zelda asked huskily when Adrien finally put the plan in front of her. 'Really serious? Because it sounds too good to be true.'

'I mean every word,' Adrien assured her. 'And the flat will have two bedrooms, so there'll be plenty of room for you and Smudge,' she added, knowing that they were currently sharing one small room with bunk beds.

'A place of our own,' Zelda whispered. 'It's like a dream. I keep waiting for someone to pinch me, and wake me up.'

The dream rapidly became a nightmare while the building work was being done. It threw up all kinds of unforeseen problems, and cost far more than anticipated. Adrien remortgaged the cottage, and raised a bank loan on the strength of her plan, while Zelda, overwhelmed at finding herself a partner, insisted on contributing the small settlement she'd received from her ex-husband.

Their faith in themselves seemed justified, she had to admit. The enquiries came in steadily from day one, and they had to rent some temporary work-space to cope with the demand. Soon they'd been in their new premises for nearly two years, and were already employing extra help with the sewing.

'Maybe we shouldn't have downsized,' Adrien joked. 'Perhaps we should have looked to expand, and put in a bid for the Grange instead.'

'Except that the Grange isn't for sale,' Zelda said, frowning over some fabric catalogues. 'What a shame—a lovely house like that, just standing empty.'

'Yes,' Adrien sighed. 'When I was a child I used to go there all the time, while my father played chess with Mr Stretton.'

'What did you do?'

Adrien shrugged. 'Oh—read books from his library, played in the garden.'

'All by yourself?'

Adrien hesitated, hearing faint alarm bells ring in her mind. 'Not all the time,' she returned. 'Mr Stretton's nephew, Piers, was there sometimes. His mother had married someone Mr Stretton disapproved of—a Brazilian—and there'd been a big row. But I suppose Mr Stretton had eventually to accept the fact that Piers was going to be his heir, and invite him to stay, although he'd still have nothing to do with his brother-in-law,' she added, frowning. 'My parents said he really hated him. Called him "a thoroughly bad lot".'

'Families.' Zelda wrinkled her nose. 'Do you think Mr Stretton will ever come back?'

'I shouldn't think so. He moved to Spain for the climate, and seems settled there.' Adrien sighed again. 'I couldn't believe it. The Grange has been in his family for years. And he'd just got to know Piers properly, too.'

'Perhaps he thought he was a bad lot as well.'

'He couldn't have done.' Adrien drew a stormy breath. 'He's one of the kindest people I ever met. Saved me from pneumonia—or hypothermia, or worse.'

Zelda put the catalogue down. 'How?'

Adrien bit her lip. 'Oh, there was a treehouse in the wood at the back of the house. I climbed up there once when I was about nine and got stuck, and he found me. But I'd been there for hours, and I was frozen and sick with fright. I'm hopeless on ladders to this day.

'But that's not all,' she added. 'When I was eighteen, Mr Stretton gave a party for me at the Grange, and he presented me with a garnet pendant, very old and very pretty. During the party it was stolen, and Piers—found it. But it was dreadful. It ruined my birthday. And he was so sweet and understanding.'

'Well, let's hear it for Piers—the hero of the hour,' Zelda said drily. 'What happened to him?'

'Oh, it was shortly afterwards that Mr Stretton closed up the house and went to live in Spain. I guess Piers went back to Brazil.'

'Shame,' said Zelda. 'By the way, who pinched the pendant?'

'One of the servants,' Adrien said shortly. 'No one important.'

Piers would be thirty-two now, she found herself thinking. And so would the other one. The one whose name she wouldn't speak. The one who'd caused all the nightmares...

Well, all that was in the past, and the past couldn't hurt her. Firmly, she slammed the gate of memory shut again, regretting that she'd allowed it to open even fractionally.

It was only ten days later that news came that Angus Stretton had died at his villa in Spain, and would be buried out there.

The vicar, however, decided to hold a memorial service at the parish church, and, to Adrien's astonishment, Piers arrived to attend it.

It was assumed locally that, having done his duty, he'd simply put the place on the market and get on with his life elsewhere.

But how wrong we were, Adrien thought—smiling to herself as she walked down the long corridor which led to the master suite.

He came—we saw each other again—and suddenly everything was different and wonderful.

She opened the door and stepped into the main bedroom. It was a large room, with doors leading to its own dressing room and a bathroom, both of them completely remodelled.

There was no furniture yet in the bedroom, which smelled of fresh paint and newly papered walls, now the colour of thick cream. The floor had been sanded and polished, and a square of deep green carpet laid.

Adrien couldn't help wishing that Piers had kept some of his uncle's furniture. Much of it was old, and she suspected valuable, and it had suited its surroundings.

But he'd insisted on a clean sweep. And since then, of course, she'd found the bed.

She'd discovered it at a country sale, lying in pieces in an outbuilding. A genuine four-poster bed, needing a lot of restoration work, admittedly, but she'd got it cheaply and handed it over to Fred Derwent, who specialised in such things and who'd received it with a delight bordering on reverence.

Soon, Adrien thought dreamily, it would be installed—the centrepiece of the room—and of their marriage.

And Zelda had unearthed some fabulous fabric, incorporating a heavily stylised pattern in blue, green and gold, from which she was making the hangings for the bed and the windows.

Three months from now, she thought, I'll be sleeping in that bed with Piers.

Happy colour rose to her face, and she laughed softly to herself.

She would still keep this morning tryst with the house, however. Only she'd wear the peignoir in ivory silk and lace that she'd bought on her last trip to London instead of the jade towelling robe which had seen better days, she thought, giving it a disparaging look.

And her dark auburn hair would be cascading over her shoulders instead of hauled up into an untidy topknot.

She would save this room until last, as she'd always done. Keeping it special. And once the new window curtains were pulled back, and she'd looked out over the wide lawns at the rear of the house, she'd go over to the bed and kiss Piers awake. And he would draw her down into the shadowed softness, back into his arms.

So far it was only a fantasy that stirred her blood and brought her senses to trembling life. But very soon now it would be reality.

She walked slowly to the window and looked out at the view she'd come to love.

And stopped, gasping, her hand flying to her mouth.

A man was standing in the middle of the expanse of grass, looking up at the house. A man dressed all in black, with an overcoat hanging from his shoulders like a cloak and early mist coiling round his legs, giving him an air of unreality, as if he'd come from another age and been caught in a time slip.

He was so still that for a moment she thought he wasn't human at all, but a statue that someone had placed there during the night as some kind of bizarre joke.

But then she saw the breeze lift the skirts of the coat and ruffle the dark blond hair, and realised that, whatever else, she was confronted by flesh and blood.

She thought, But not Piers, and her heart plummeted, shock replaced by disappointment. Piers wasn't quite as tall as the figure below, and his hair was raven-dark. And yet— just for a second—she'd experienced this curious sense of familiarity.

Who is he? she asked herself. And what is he doing here?

The Grange had its share of visitors, most of them driven by curiosity to see how the work was progressing. But they didn't come at sunrise, and usually they asked first.

Adrien swallowed. A visitor who came unannounced this early in the day had to be an intruder. Someone who was up to no good. A potential burglar casing the place? she wondered frantically. She'd heard of empty houses being stripped to the bone, their fixtures and fittings carried off. And downstairs there was a brand-new kitchen, as well as Angus Stretton's library, its walls still lined with books.

She said fiercely under her breath, 'But this house isn't empty. And you're not taking anything.'

She turned and ran to the door, tearing along the corridor to the wide oak staircase, launching herself downwards.

The drawing room was also at the rear of the house, to take advantage of the view, and French windows led on to the terrace. She ran towards them, grabbing the keys from the pocket of her robe.

It was the stark chill of the stone flags under her bare feet that startled her into awareness of what she was doing. She hesitated, staring around her, scanning the now-deserted lawn, recognising that the black-clad intruder was nowhere to be seen.

And at the same time she heard in the distance the sound of a departing car. He must, she thought, have parked at the side of the house, where he wouldn't be seen. But how had he known that?

Adrien realised she was holding her breath, and released it, gulping as common sense belatedly intervened.

What on earth did she think she was doing? she asked herself. Charging down here like a maniac, with only a bunch of keys for protection. Quite apart from wearing nothing except an elderly robe. Hardly confrontation gear, she acknowledged, tightening the belt protectively round her slim waist. And just as well the stranger had disappeared.

But why the hell hadn't she stayed in the house and used her mobile phone to call for assistance? How could she possibly have taken such a stupid risk?

After all, he could have been violent, and she might have ended up badly injured, or worse.

He must have assumed she wasn't alone, or else he'd have stood his ground.

Because he'd known she was there. She was convinced of it. Certain that he'd seen her, somehow, standing in the window. And that his dark figure had stiffened.

But that's crazy, she thought, beginning to shake inwardly at the realisation of her narrow escape. He couldn't possibly have picked me out from that distance. I'd have simply been another shadow inside the house.

And I couldn't have noticed such a detail either. I'm letting my imagination run away with me.

She straightened her shoulders and stepped back into the drawing room.

It was over, she reassured herself, and nothing had happened. But she would play safe and report the incident to the local police station, although there wasn't much they could do without a detailed description of a car number.

He'd invaded her privacy, she thought, as she trailed back upstairs to shower and dress. Spoiled that first golden hour of her day. Made her feel edgy and ill at ease, as if a storm was brewing.

Oh, pull yourself together, she adjured herself impatiently. You're reacting like a spoiled child. And you'll have tomorrow and all the days to come to treasure, so you're hardly deprived.

And he was probably some poor soul who'd been driving all night and had turned in at the wrong gate through tiredness.

She gave a small, fierce nod, and turned on the shower.

She dressed for action, in a tee shirt under a pair of denim dungarees, and secured her hair at the nape of her neck with an elastic band.

Over a breakfast of toast and coffee, she reviewed what the workmen would be doing when they arrived, making notes on her clipboard as she ate.

There was some tiling to complete round the new Aga in the kitchen, and plumbing to install in the laundry room. They'd converted the old flower room into a downstairs cloakroom, and if the plaster was dry that could be painted. The panelling in the dining room was finished, but the ceiling needed another coat of emulsion.

Most of the bedrooms were finished, apart from the one

with the camp bed that she was occupying at the front of the house.

She decided she would make a start on that, peeling off the layers of old wallpaper with the steam stripper. It was a messy process, but she enjoyed it.

Remembering how immaculately the house had been kept in Mr Stretton's time, Adrien could have wept when Piers had taken her back there to see what needed to be done. The plaster had been flaking, and there had been damp patches on some upstairs ceilings. In addition, her practised nose had warned her that dry rot was present.

'My God,' Piers had muttered. 'It might be easier just to pull the place down.'

'No.' She'd squeezed his hand. 'We'll make it beautiful again. You'll see.'

And she'd been as good as her word, she reflected, with satisfaction. The Grange was looking pretty wonderful already. Most of the work that was left was cosmetic—adding finishing touches—so that the final bills should be relatively modest.

At least compared with the last batch that she'd just paid, she remembered, shuddering.

She was making good progress with the steam stripper when it occurred to her that her small workforce was uncharacteristically late. She finished the section she was working on, then unclipped her mobile from the belt of her jeans.

But before she could dial it rang, making her jump and swear under her breath.

She said crisply, 'A to Z Design. Good morning.'

'Is that Miss Lander?' It was the boss of the building firm she was using. 'It's Gordon Arnold here.'

She gave a sigh of relief. 'I was just about to call you, Gordon. No one's turned up yet. Is there some reason?'

'You could say that.' His voice was slow and deliberate. 'We've had a bit of a problem.'

Not another vehicle breakdown, Adrien thought with a faint irritation. Gordon should get himself a van that worked.

She said briskly, 'Well, try to get it sorted quickly. There's still plenty to do here.'

'That's it, you see, Miss Lander.' He sounded odd, embarrassed. 'We did the work, and you paid us for it, same as always. Except this time the bank sent the cheques back.'

Adrien was very still for a moment. This was a room that caught the early sun, yet she felt suddenly deathly cold.

Rallying herself, she said, 'There must be some mistake.'

'That's exactly what I said.' He sounded almost eager. 'A mistake. So I got on to the bank, but they wouldn't talk to me. Said I had to refer to you.'

Adrien groaned. 'I'll get on to them myself,' she said. 'It'll probably be a computer error,' she added confidently.

'Dare say it will,' he said. 'Generally is. I'll leave it with you, then, Miss Lander. Only, we can't really do any more work until we know we're going to be paid, and there's other jobs waiting.'

'Yes, of course,' she said. 'I'll have it put right by this afternoon, Gordon. Cheers.'

But she didn't feel very cheery as she switched off the phone and put it back on her belt.

Something had gone badly wrong, she thought, as she went to her room to retrieve her bag and, because she was still feeling cold, a jacket.

It was a mistake. It had to be. Yet somehow she kept getting an image of that dark, silent figure standing unmoving in front of the house, like some symbol of ill omen.

Don't be silly, Adie, she reproved herself, using the childish version of her name she'd coined when she was small. Just go to the bank and get it sorted.

It was a simple enough system that she and Piers had devised. He'd opened an account at a local bank, with a chequebook in her name, and each month she sent him an itemised account of her spending and he deposited sufficient funds to cover it.

'You're too trusting,' she'd told him.

'I love you,' he'd returned. 'Love can't trust too much.'

For the past four months the system had worked like a charm. But this time, when some of the heaviest bills had to be paid, a hiccup had developed.

I suppose it had to happen eventually, Adrien thought, as she set her Jeep in motion. Nothing's perfect, especially when it's automated. But why did it have to be this month?

The bank was busy, but as Adrien waited at the enquiry desk she had the curious feeling that people were watching her. That a couple of the cashiers had exchanged glances as she walked in.

They probably realise they've screwed up in a big way and are wondering how to apologise, she decided, with an inward shrug.

The enquiry clerk looked nonplussed when she saw her. 'Oh—Miss Lander. The manager has been trying to contact you at home, but we only got your answer-machine.'

'That's right.' Adrien's brows lifted in slight hauteur. My God, she thought, she sounds almost accusing. 'I'm staying at the Grange so that I can oversee the final stages.' If it's any business of yours.

'Oh—that explains it. Will you take a seat for a few moments? Mr Davidson needs to talk to you urgently.'

Adrien was glad to sit down, because her legs were trembling suddenly and her stomach was quaking.

Because those were not phrases that indicated grovelling on the bank's part. On the contrary...

She wished that she'd taken the trouble to change, to put on a skirt and blouse, or even a dress, some heels, and some make-up. Because she had the oddest feeling she was going to need all the help she could get. She was also aware that in her present gear she looked about sixteen.

'Miss Lander?' Mr Davidson was standing beside her. 'Come into the interview room, won't you?' His smile was pallid and his gaze slid away. A very different reaction from his enthusiasm when the account was being set up.

She wished, not for the first time, that Piers had used her own bank, where she was a known and valued customer.

While he closed the door, Adrien took the chair he indicated. 'Mr Davidson, I understand you've returned some of my cheques.'

'I've had no choice, Miss Lander. There are no funds to meet them.'

Her throat tightened, and her heart began to pound. She heard herself say with unbelievable calmness, 'Then payment must have been delayed for some reason. Perhaps you could give me a little leeway here, while I contact my fiancé.'

'I'm afraid not, Miss Lander. You see, we've been notified that no further deposits will be made. Did Mr Mendoza not warn you of his intentions?'

'No more deposits?' Her lips felt numb. 'But that's impossible.'

'I fear not.' He paused, as if choosing his words carefully. 'I have some other bad news which I must pass on to you. I have just learned that Mr Mendoza is no longer the owner of Wildhurst Grange. That he has sold it to a property development company.'

There was a strange buzzing in Adrien's ears. The room seemed to be swimming round her.

She said hoarsely, 'No—it's not true. It can't be. He—he wouldn't do that. Not without telling me—discussing it…'

'I'm afraid it is perfectly true. I have the head of the

company in my office now, and…Miss Lander—where are you going?'

The metal handle slipped in her damp grip, but she wrenched the door open and ran out.

The door to the manager's office had been left slightly ajar. She pushed it wide and went in, knowing what she was going to see. Fearing it…

A man was standing by the window. He was tall, and dressed in beautifully cut black Italian trousers and a matching rollneck sweater in fine wool. The long overcoat had been discarded, and was lying across a chair. His dark blond hair, expertly layered, reached the collar of his sweater. His face was lean, with a beak of a nose and strongly marked mouth and chin. The eyes that met hers across the room were as grey as a northern sea, and about as warm.

And at the edge of one cheekbone there was a small triangular scar.

Adrien recognised that scar, because she'd put it there. She'd been just nine years old, and she had been cold, hungry, and hysterical. Because he'd deliberately left her on a flimsy platform in a tall tree for hours. To punish her. To make her think that she'd be left there for ever. That she'd die there.

So she'd picked up a stone, and flung it at him. He'd gasped and thrown back his head, but it had hit him, and she had seen a small trickle of blood on his face and been glad, because she'd hated him. She'd wanted to hurt him.

He'd looked at her then with those cold grey eyes just as he was looking at her now. With contempt and a kind of icy arrogance. And without pity.

She'd been frightened then, and she was frightened now. Too scared to speak or to run. Although she was no longer a child. Or an eighteen-year-old whose birthday had been ruined by theft and betrayal.

All these years she'd blotted him out of her memory, even though the legacy of those traumatic days was still with her. Haunting her each time she had to climb a ladder or stand on a chair, and found herself assailed by nausea and giddiness. Piercing her when she opened her jewellery drawer and saw the empty velvet box which had once held the garnet pendant.

But she'd managed to convince herself that she would never see him again. That she could bury the past.

And that he would have done the same.

But she was wrong, because here he was.

And once again she was stranded and terrified, with no means of escape.

CHAPTER TWO

'IT's been a long time, Adrien.' His voice had deepened, but she would have recognised that husky timbre anywhere.

She would not—*not*—allow herself to go to pieces in front of him. Not again. Not for a third time.

Instead she lifted her chin defiantly. 'My God.' She kept her tone just this side of insolence. 'It's the Haddon boy.'

'No,' he said. 'Not any longer. I've become the Haddon man. A distinction I advise you to observe.'

'A threat,' she said. 'But then you were always good at them.'

'And an accusation,' he said. 'For which you had a positive genius. Even when you were in pigtails. And later.' The grey eyes made a leisurely and nerve-jangling inspection of her. 'You haven't changed a great deal—over the intervening years.'

Her throat tightened. 'I'm afraid I can't say the same for you. I would never have known you.'

He laughed softly. 'Are you quite sure about that, Adie? Wasn't there just a glimmer of recognition this morning when you were staring down at me from your ivory tower?'

His use of her childhood name grated. As did the confirmation of her earlier suspicion that he'd known she was there.

She said shortly, 'You were the last person in the world I ever expected to see again. And you didn't hang around to introduce yourself.'

'No,' he said. 'I had business elsewhere. And besides, I knew we'd be meeting again very soon. I didn't want to anticipate such a pleasurable moment. The first, I hope, of so many more to come,' he added silkily.

She bit her lip. 'So—what are you doing here? Why have you come back? I don't understand...'

'You're not required to.' His smile chafed her nerve-endings. 'Perhaps I just wanted to surprise you.'

He looked past her as Mr Davidson peered anxiously into the room.

'Is everything all right, Mr Haddon?'

'Everything's fine, thanks.' The sudden switch to power and charm made Adrien reel inwardly. 'Could you give us five minutes? Miss Lander and I would like to renew our old acquaintance.'

'Yes—yes—of course.' Mr Davidson began to back out of the room.

She wanted to cry out, Don't go. Don't leave me with him. But she couldn't allow herself to betray such weakness.

Instead, she stood in silence and watched the door close. Shutting her in with him. Her enemy.

'How very deferential of him,' she threw into the sudden silence. 'I'm surprised he didn't call you sir.'

'He probably will—given time. I'm about to become a very important customer at this bank.'

'Does he know you were the housekeeper's son?' She cringed inwardly at the crudity of the query. Despised herself for voicing it too. Because she'd liked Mrs Haddon, who'd always been warm and kind to her on Adrien's visits to the Grange with her father.

She had a sudden memory of the well-scrubbed kitchen table, being allowed to scrape the remains of the cake mixture from the bowl. And being given fresh-baked cookies, with her initial picked out in chocolate chips.

'I've no idea.' His voice was calm. 'But it would make

no difference. Because money talks—and it has a louder voice than your outdated notions of snobbery.'

Faint colour rose in her face, but she stood her ground. 'Then you've come up in the world. How odd.'

His brows lifted. 'I've worked hard. I've found it pays off. And I intend to go on working so I can have what I want in life.'

'Wildhurst Grange, for instance?'

'Among other things, yes.'

'Well, I don't believe it,' she said. 'Piers would never sell his inheritance—and especially not to you.'

'Piers would sell his own grandmother to get out of the kind of mess he's in.'

She said thickly, 'How dare you say that? After the way you've behaved. You always hated him—you were always jealous...'

'I had no reason to like him.' The grey eyes glittered at her. 'But I wasn't jealous. He had nothing that I wanted—not then.'

'And now you want the Grange. So you've stolen it from him—somehow.' She lifted her chin contemptuously. 'Well—once a thief, always a thief.'

'What a depressingly commonplace mind you've developed, Adie,' he drawled. 'It must be through associating with Mr Mendoza. But I'm sure you'll recover.'

'I don't have to,' she said. 'Or did you think I'd dump Piers because he doesn't have the Grange any more?' She moistened her dry lips with the tip of her tongue. 'If so, you're wrong. Because that was never the attraction. Piers and I are going to be together, no matter what's gone wrong. As soon as I get home I'm going to call him and...'

'Well, make sure you get the time zones right.' He looked at his watch. 'It's probably the middle of the night in Brazil. And you wouldn't want to disturb him on his honeymoon.'

The sudden silence in the room was almost tangible. Adrien could feel it beating against her eardrums, constricting her heart.

She looked at him numbly. He seemed to have retreated to a great distance, his dark figure swimming in front of her. Swimming...

'Sit down.' His voice was suddenly incisive, authoritative. 'Put your head between your knees and breathe deeply.'

She obeyed for no better reason than her legs no longer seemed capable of supporting her.

When the dizziness had passed, and she could speak again, she said, 'You're lying.'

He said slowly, 'No, it's true. He'd been seeing this girl out in Portugal, and made her pregnant. Her father is Brazilian, and powerful, and insisted on marriage. And Brazil was a safer option for him than London or Lisbon.'

He paused. 'Will you believe, Adrien, that it gives me no pleasure to tell you?'

'No.' She raised her head to glare at him. 'I don't believe it. You've waited a long time for your revenge, Chay Haddon. Waited to punish me for having you sent away all those years ago. I just wish with all my heart that you'd gone to jail instead.'

'Only to jail?' he came back at her mockingly. 'I was certain hell would be the preferred destination.'

'Hell's too good for you.' She pushed back a strand of hair that had escaped its confinement and got to her feet, swaying slightly as she fought off the last remnants of dizziness.

'Be careful.' He went to take her arm, and she recoiled.

'Don't touch me,' she said hoarsely. 'Don't ever *dare* to touch me.'

'A threat, an accusation, and now a challenge.' He was actually smiling. 'What a pity I have neither the time nor the inclination to take you up on it. At present,' he added silkily. 'I gather you're terminating our reunion. May I ask where you're going?'

'Yes,' she said. 'I'm going to find Piers and talk to him. Show you up for the liar and cheat that you are.'

'I wouldn't have so much to say about cheating.' There was a note of grimness in his voice. 'Not when you owe money all over the area. And don't even think of going to Brazil, Adie, always supposing you could find the fare. I'm sure your creditors wouldn't like it, quite apart from Piers's wife.'

He opened the door and held it for her. 'I'll see you around.'

To answer, Not if I see you first, would have been simply childish rudeness. Instead Adrien did not even glance at him as she walked out of the office.

She heard Mr Davidson saying, 'Miss Lander—Miss Lander, I need to talk to you,' but she ignored him too, breaking into a run as she headed for the door of the bank.

She could only think of Piers, and the necessity to contact him. To disprove the monstrous things that Chay Haddon had been saying. Nothing else mattered, or could be allowed to matter.

The next hour was a nightmare. She tried faxing Piers in Portugal, but found his outlet had been closed down and that the same thing applied to his e-mail address. The telephone line she'd always used seemed to be disconnected.

Panic was closing her throat and making her fingers clumsy as she pressed the buttons on her receiver, trying every number he'd ever given her.

Eventually someone answered—a man speaking Portuguese. She asked haltingly for Piers, and heard him say something in a muffled voice, as if he'd covered the phone with his hand, which was followed by a burst of laughter, as if other people in the room were responding to his remark. To a joke that her query had triggered.

Adrien found she had bitten her lip so hard she could taste blood.

When he spoke to her directly, he made her understand in fractured English that Piers had gone to Brazil and would not be coming back. Nor could he tell her where she could contact him.

Amid another shout of laughter, he added, 'Good luck.'

She put the receiver back on its stand and stared into space, aware that her heart was thudding erratically against her ribcage.

However unacceptable she might find it, it seemed that Chay Haddon had been speaking the truth after all. That Piers had indeed sold him the Grange, and vanished.

She could feel pain ready to explode inside her, but she dammed it back. She could not deal with her personal anguish and betrayal now, because there were other overriding considerations.

Thanks to Piers, she was now in debt for thousands of pounds, over and above her mortgage and bank loan. All over the area there were people who would soon be demanding their money, and she had no means of paying them.

She looked around her at the pleasant sitting room, with its familiar furniture and ornaments. They'd always been part of her life, but soon all of them could be lost for ever, along with the cottage, and the business.

She was without illusions about what she could be facing. Bankruptcy was staring her in the face, and it would touch everyone around her too. Zelda and Smudge could end up homeless. And there were the women in the workroom as well, who thought they were in secure employment and had taken on extra obligations as a result.

And all because she'd fallen in love.

A sob rose in her throat.

She'd trusted Piers and he'd defaulted, crudely and cruelly. Her name was on the empty account and the cheque-book, and she was responsible. She had no contract or written guarantees. Nothing that could support her in law, even if Piers could be found.

He'd arranged it that way, quite deliberately, and because she loved him she'd agreed. And her naivety could cost her everything.

And it wasn't as if she hadn't been warned. Zelda had been openly unhappy about taking on such a big project that would absorb all Adrien's time and energy.

'People aren't going to wait while you sort out the Grange,' she'd argued. 'They'll go elsewhere. Tell people we're never available. And word soon gets round. We shouldn't put all our eggs in one basket like this.'

But she'd wanted to be totally involved in the Grange's restoration, she thought achingly, because it was going to be her home, and she didn't want anyone else imposing their ideas. Intruding on the idyll she was creating.

Moving like an automaton, she went through to the kitchen, filled the kettle and set it on the stove to boil. She needed some strong black coffee to clear her head while she made a list. She needed to know the entire extent of her obligations and also what work A to Z had in the pipe-line.

She would also have to go back and face Mr Davidson, as well as her own bank manager. Try and arrange an over-draft facility or a further loan. And then work her way out of trouble.

She swallowed, aware that she had a hard furrow to plough.

But she had to start somewhere. See if she could pull some of the irons out of the fire before Zelda and the others got to hear the rumours that would already be flying...

They depend on me, and I can't let them down, she thought, catching her breath convulsively. I can't...

She fetched a notepad and a pencil and began to write.

In spite of her brave front, backed up by business suit and briefcase, all her worst fears had been confirmed by mid-afternoon.

Her own bank manager, while sympathetic, had told her that her borrowing limit was already fully extended, and he couldn't agree another loan. And Mr Davidson had sighed heavily, looking down his nose, and had asked how she proposed to pay off her present unauthorised overdraft.

Even more dauntingly, both of them had recommended her to consult an insolvency expert 'without delay'.

She had also been reminded that, as the Grange now belonged to Haddon Developments, she was in effect squatting, and should remove her personal effects immediately and hand over her keys to Mr Haddon's lawyers, Frencham and Co, in the High Street.

So there was no reprieve, Adrien thought as she climbed wearily back into her Jeep. And the execution would take place as scheduled. She was shaking inwardly, and her facial muscles ached from the effort of hanging on to her self-control.

In a few short hours she had been transformed from a girl happily in charge of her own life, with a successful business and a future with the man she loved, into some kind of grotesque puppet, capable of movement only when someone else jerked the strings.

And the worst part of it all—the realisation that flayed her skin and made her stomach quiver with nausea—was that Chay Haddon was the one holding the strings.

And each time she'd encountered him he'd brought trauma with him, she thought shivering.

What in the world could have brought him back? That

was what she couldn't understand. Because his own memories of the Grange could hardly be happy ones. The housekeeper's son, she thought, who'd been sent off to boarding school for marooning her in a tree, then banished from the house for ever for stealing her garnet pendant.

Was he seeking some kind of posthumous revenge on Angus Stretton, who'd been responsible for exiling him from the house and had also, in the aftermath, sacked his mother, who'd given such quiet and faithful service for so many years.

If so, there was a real sickness there, she thought, wrapping her arms protectively around her body.

But it was a comprehensive and sweeping retribution that he was exacting. Piers had lost his inheritance, and she— she was facing financial ruin.

As he was already well aware, she realised, recalling his jibe about her creditors. He knew exactly what he was doing. The thief had returned as a robber baron, and this time he'd stolen her whole life.

She wanted to run and hide. Seek some dark corner where no one would ever find her. But she couldn't do that. She had to be strong—to stand her ground and fight back with whatever weapons she could get.

But first she had to say farewell to the Grange. She still couldn't deal with the more personal loss, although she'd have to do so soon. She'd have to admit that Piers had deserted her and married someone else. Endure the inevitable gossip and speculation. Local people were kind, but only human, and her downfall would be sensational stuff. Plus, there would be resentment from those who'd worked on the Grange, and were owed money as a result.

When businesses went bust there was often a knock-on effect, and the local economy couldn't afford it, she thought worriedly.

Gordon and his sub-contractors would be the main victims.

I'll pay them back somehow, she vowed silently. Even it takes the rest of my life.

A life that stretched before her as bleak and empty as a desert—and, she realised, with a pang, just as dangerous.

The Grange looked beautiful in the late-afternoon sun, the mellow brickwork glowing.

Adrien swallowed past the sudden constriction in her throat and drove round to the side of the house.

To her limitless relief, there were no other vehicles around.

Don't look too closely at anything, she adjured herself, as she left the Jeep. You can't afford to be emotional. Not yet. Just grab your things and get out while the going's good.

Usually when she walked across the wide entrance hall, and up the sweep of oak staircase, she felt all the pride of ownership glowing inside her. Today she couldn't even afford a glimmer of satisfaction in a job well done.

Because Chay Haddon wasn't just getting a house. He was getting all the heart and soul that she'd poured into it. All the love.

And she was only sorry she couldn't tear it down, brick by brick, with her bare hands, and leave him with a pile of rubble.

Instead she was the one with the handful of dust—and the nightmares.

She walked slowly to the side door and stood for a moment, trying to control her flurried breathing. She had the key in her hand, so what was she waiting for?

She needed to go in—to get the whole thing over and done with—then be on her way. For the last time.

Gagging suddenly, she turned and ran, stumbling in her

haste. She by-passed the lawn, where Chay Haddon had stood that morning, opting for the gravelled path which led to what had once been the enclosed kitchen garden but which now resembled a jungle on a bad day.

She closed her mind to the plans she'd made to transform this riot of weeds into a thriving vegetable plot again and kept running, until she reached the gate at the far end, and the area of woodland beyond it.

It was so long since she'd been here. She'd deliberately shunned this part of the grounds for sixteen years. But now, in the face of the greatest crisis of her life, she needed to confront that old childhood fear and defeat it.

She was looking for the only oak tree—an ancient, massive specimen, with room in its spreading branches for a whole terrace of treehouses.

'*So where does he go all day?*' Down the years, Piers's voice returned to haunt her. '*The housekeeper's son. Where does he hide himself? Do you know?*'

And she, eager to please this glamorous dark-haired boy, paying his first visit to his uncle, had said, 'Yes—I'll show you.' At the same time knowing, guiltily, that she shouldn't. That it was not her secret to share.

Now, for a moment, staring up into the branches, she thought she'd picked the wrong tree. She'd been convinced that time would roll back, and she'd find herself, just nine years old, in shorts and tee shirt, her hair in the plaits she'd hated, looking up longingly at the wooden platform that had been Chay's hidden place.

An elderly ladder had been propped against the lower trunk, and after that you'd climbed up through the branches until you reached the treehouse.

It had had a roof of sorts, and three walls constructed out of timber oddments, but to Adrien it had been a magic place—a castle, a palace, a cave where anything could happen.

She had known, because he'd let her look through his binoculars, that Chay went there to watch birds mostly, but sometimes he'd come to read or just think. He'd kept books up there, and a sketchpad, and a tin of biscuits.

She'd asked once, 'Isn't it funny—being all on your own here?'

He'd looked at her thoughtfully, not smiling. 'It's good to be alone sometimes. You need to be comfortable in your own company before you can be happy with other people.'

Adrien hadn't been sure what he meant, and her face must have shown it, because he'd laughed suddenly, and reached out, tugging gently at a plait.

'Is it so awful, Adie—the thought of having no one to talk to?'

'I'd hate it,' she'd said, shivering as a breeze stirred the leaves and made them sigh. 'I'd be frightened. Up here by myself.'

I actually told him that, she thought. I put the weapon in his hand and he used it against me. Used it to punish me. Unforgettably. Unforgivably.

There was no ladder there now, or platform, no flapping roof. No trace of the little girl who'd knelt there, crying, for all that endless time, convinced she'd been deserted and forgotten.

It was just—a tree.

His voice reached her quietly. 'It's been gone a long time, Adie. Angus had the gardener dismantle it and put it on a bonfire. I had to watch it burn.'

She spun round, her hand flying to her mouth. 'What are you doing here?' She'd had no inkling of his approach until he spoke.

'You have a short memory,' he said. 'I own the place now—remember?' He looked her over, absorbing the dark grey linen suit and the white silk camisole beneath it. 'What happened to this morning's Pollyanna?'

She said shortly, 'Pollyanna grew up—fast. And I meant how did you know where I'd be? Because I never come here.'

'Your Jeep was there,' he said. 'But the doors were still locked. I—obeyed an instinct.'

She supposed she had done the same thing, and it irked her. She lifted her chin. 'I'm—trespassing. I apologise. I came to clear out my stuff.'

He glanced round, brows raised. 'You've been camping in the wood?' he enquired. 'How enterprising.'

'No,' she said. 'It's in the house. I—I'll go and fetch it—if that's all right.'

He shrugged. 'Be my guest.'

She offered him a frozen smile. 'I think that's carrying hospitality too far.'

'As it happens,' he said slowly, 'you've already been under my roof for nearly a week.'

She swallowed, forcing her legs to move, walking back down the track. 'The sale went through that long ago? And I wasn't told? Oh, but I suppose it all happened in Portugal.'

'No,' he said. 'I was in London, and so was Piers. He came over to sign the necessary papers before leaving for Brazil.'

For a moment she couldn't speak. She certainly couldn't move as she digested this latest blow.

Piers had been in England, she thought with anguish, and she hadn't known. He'd been here, and he hadn't warned her. She wanted to sink to her knees and howl her misery to the sky.

Chay watched her. He said, 'Obviously he didn't make contact.'

It was a statement, not a question. But then, he'd been able to observe her shock and desperation at close quarters earlier that day. He knew how brutal the deception had been.

Adrien straightened her shoulders and set off again. She said coolly, 'That's understandable. After all, I might have taken it badly—learning I'd been jilted as well as saddled with a mountain of debt. Far better to let me find out once he was at a safe distance. I suppose Brazil could be considered a safe distance. Besides, he knew what fun you'd have, breaking the news to me in person.'

His mouth twisted. 'You have a weird idea of what I find enjoyable. But I'll say this for you, Adie, you're not a whinger.'

'Give me time,' she tossed back over her shoulder. 'I'm planning a whinge of cosmic proportions. Would you like to buy a ticket? It seems I need every penny I can get. And you don't have to follow me,' she added with aggression. 'I'm not planning to rob the place.'

'Don't be paranoid,' he said. 'We just happen to be going in the same direction.'

'No,' she said forcefully. 'No, we don't. Not now, not ever. Could you wait somewhere, please, while I collect my things? Then I'll be out of your face.'

'Sorry.' He shook his head. 'I want to look over the Grange—see what's been done and what's left to do.'

'I have the whole thing on computer,' she said. 'I'll send you a print-out.'

'It might be useful.' He was walking beside her now. The track was narrow, and it was difficult to avoid contact with him. 'But I'd prefer a guided tour and a detailed break-down of the renovations process from the person respon-sible. You.'

She halted, lips parting in a gasp of outrage. She'd trans-formed the Grange for Piers and herself. Her hopes and dreams were woven intimately into the fabric of each room.

Too intimately to share with an interloper. She felt as if he'd asked her to strip naked.

She said jerkily, 'I have a better idea. Hire another design team and let them fill in the missing pieces. Although you could probably sell it as it stands, if you want a fast profit.'

He gave her a hooded look. 'What makes you think I'm going to sell?'

My accountant, she thought. She'd telephoned him earlier—asked, trying to sound casual, what he knew about Haddon Developments.

Chay, she'd learned, was a mover and shaker. 'His speciality,' Mark had told her, 'is identifying major building projects that have run into financial difficulties, buying them for bottom dollar, then selling them on after completion for megabucks. He's good at it. Why are you asking?'

'Oh,' she'd said. 'Someone was mentioning his name, that's all.'

Mark had laughed. 'Friend or foe?' he'd enquired. 'Word has it he's a good man to have on your side, but a bad one to cross. Generally he doesn't arouse lukewarm opinions.'

She'd said lightly, 'Thanks for the warning.' Adding silently, It's only sixteen years too late.

Now, she looked back at her adversary. 'Because that's what you do. You move in, clean up, and move on.'

'Not always,' he said. 'And not this time. Because I'm going to live here.'

'But you can't.' The words escaped before she could stop them.

'Why not?'

'You already have somewhere to live.' Mark again. 'You have a flat in a converted warehouse by the Thames, and a farmhouse in Suffolk.'

'You've really done your homework,' he said appreciatively. 'When interior design palls, you could always apply to MI5.'

She shrugged. 'Local boy makes good. That's always news. Even if it's the housekeeper's son.'

'Especially when it's the housekeeper's son,' he said mockingly.

She glared at him, and walked on. When he spoke again his voice was quiet, 'I was sorry to hear about your parents, Adie. I know how close you all were.'

She said tightly, 'Clearly I'm not the only one to do homework.' And they completed the rest of the walk back to the house in silence.

Outside the side door, Adrien paused and drew a deep breath. 'If you want to make your inspection in privacy, I can come back another day for my things.'

'No,' he said. 'Get them now. That is, if you're sure you won't come round with me.'

'I'm certain.'

'Don't you want to boast of your achievements?'

She shrugged. 'I don't feel particularly triumphant. Anyway, you're the expert,' she added with edge. 'I don't need to point out a thing.'

'You used to like company.'

'That,' she said, 'would depend on the company. I'll see myself out when I've finished.'

Once inside, she headed for the stairs, and the room she'd been using. She hadn't brought much, and her travel bag was soon packed. She was just rolling up the sleeping bag she'd been using when Chay appeared in the doorway.

'So you chose this room?' He looked round, brows raised quizzically as he took in the narrow camp bed. 'I'd have thought the master bedroom was the appropriate place for the mistress. Don't you find this a little cramped for passion? Or did Piers like you to keep still?'

Her face flamed. 'You bastard. You know nothing about it—nothing. Piers and I were engaged.'

His glance skimmed her bare left hand. 'Really? Well,

at least you don't have to send the ring back for—er, re-cycling.'

There was a silence, then she said huskily, 'That was an unforgivable thing to say.'

'Yes,' he said. 'But so much between us, my sweet, has been unforgivable. And unforgiven.'

She snatched up the travel bag and walked towards the door which he was still blocking.

She said, 'Will you let me pass, please?'

'In a moment. I have a proposal to put to you.'

My God, Adrien thought. He's going to ask me to finish the house.

Naturally, she would refuse. It would break her heart to go on working here, with all the might-have-beens. Yet—if she agreed—she could charge him a fee that would enable her to start paying her creditors. Could she really afford to turn down such a chance?

She said discouragingly, 'Well?'

Before she could guess what he was going to do, or take evasive action, his hands had slid under the lapels of her jacket, pushing them apart, while the grey eyes made a slow, lingering survey of the swell of her rounded breasts under the clinging camisole.

He said softly, 'Very well. Quite exquisite, in fact. You've grown up beautifully, Adie.'

'Don't call me that.' Shaken to the core by the sudden unprovoked intimacy, she pulled away, horrified to realise that behind their silken barrier her nipples were hardening in swift, shamed excitement.

'And don't handle me either,' she added, her voice quivering. 'You have no right...'

His mouth twisted unrepentantly. 'Not even the *droit de seigneur*?'

'You bought a house,' she said. 'I was not included in the price. Now, let me past.'

'Only because Piers didn't think of it.' His voice was reflective, and he made no attempt to move. 'But as you've raised the subject, Adrien, what value do you put on your services?'

She said slowly, hardly daring to hope, 'Are you offering to pay for the work I've done?'

'That would rather depend,' he drawled. 'You see, it occurs to me that this house lacks something. And so do I.'

She drew a deep breath. 'You mean that it isn't quite finished. But it wouldn't take much...'

'No,' he said. 'That isn't what I mean at all.'

'Then what?' she asked defensively, hating the way his grey gaze held hers, yet somehow unable to look away. Or walk away.

'It needs a mistress,' he said softly. 'And so do I. And you, my sweet Adrien, are the perfect candidate. So, maybe we can do a deal. What do you say?'

CHAPTER THREE

SHE said thickly, 'Is this some kind of sick joke?'

'Do you see me laughing?'

No, she thought, swallowing. The grey eyes meeting hers in challenge were cool, direct—even insolent. The firm mouth was equally unsmiling. No—it seemed he was shockingly—incredibly—serious.

'So you're just adding insult to injury.' She tried to laugh, but the sound choked in her throat. 'Time hasn't mellowed you, Chay. You're still a bastard.'

He smiled. '"Now, gods, stand up for bastards!"' he quoted softly. 'However, I see myself more as a white knight riding to your rescue.'

'Very chivalrous.' Her voice bit.

'No,' he said. 'I'm a businessman. You claim to be a businesswoman, and you're in financial trouble. I'm offering you a lifeline.' His gaze touched her parted lips and travelled down to her breasts. 'A very personal loan,' he added softly.

Adrien bit her lip. She said savagely, 'Mr Davidson needs to learn some discretion.'

'Mr Davidson didn't tell me a thing.' Chay propped a shoulder against the doorframe. 'He didn't have to. I could sense the shock waves as soon as I arrived. And when I was here earlier today, a plasterer and an electrician turned up waving major bills which had been refused payment. I'd make an educated guess that they're just the tip of the iceberg. That you're facing serious trouble.'

Adrien lifted her chin. 'And if I am,' she said curtly, 'I'll manage. I can survive without your particular brand of knight errantry.'

'Then I wish you luck,' Chay said silkily. 'But I hope you're not counting on a bank draft arriving from Brazil. You'd do better to rely on the National Lottery.'

'You utter swine,' she said unevenly. 'You've got everything you've wanted, haven't you? How you must be enjoying your moment of triumph.'

'I've had to wait long enough,' he said. 'But they say that revenge is a dish best eaten cold.'

'I hope it poisons you,' she flung at him. 'Now let me out of here.'

He straightened. Moved out of the doorway. 'You're not a prisoner,' he pointed out mildly.

'No,' she said. 'Nor do I intend to be, either.'

'Do you imagine I'm going to keep you chained up like some sort of sex slave?' He had the gall to sound amused. 'What a vivid imagination you have, darling.'

'Don't you dare laugh at me.' Her voice shook. 'You can't pretend what you're suggesting is a normal arrangement.'

'On the contrary, very little in your life would change.' He sounded the soul of reason, she thought incredulously.

'After all, you're already living here,' he went on.

'That,' she said swiftly, 'was just a temporary convenience.'

'Which would become a permanent one.' The return was incisive. 'But you'd have your debts paid, plus a free hand to finish the house exactly as you want, and staff to manage it for you. You'd go on running your business quite independently. And when I have guests you'd act as my hostess.'

'And that's all there is to it?' Adrien enquired ironically.

'No,' he said equably. 'My work takes me abroad a great

deal. I'd expect you to accompany me sometimes. But not always.' He paused. 'I take it your passport's in order?'

'Of course,' she said, staring at him. 'And this conversation is totally surreal.'

'Before commencing any project I like to establish the ground rules,' he said silkily. 'When I'm away, you'll be free to come and go as you please. Entertain your own friends. Live your life.'

'It sounds too good to be true,' she said. 'Which of course it is. Because when these business trips were over, you'd come back.'

'Naturally.' He was smiling faintly.

'Expecting precisely what?'

'You're no longer a child, Adrien.' There was a sudden harshness in his voice. 'Or a romantic teenager, dreaming of first love. I'd expect you to fulfil your side of the deal.'

'Just the idea,' she said, 'makes me physically sick.'

'Once,' he said slowly, 'you didn't feel like that.'

'What do you mean?' She stiffened defensively.

'It was your birthday,' he said. 'You were eighteen, and you looked as if someone had lit stars behind your eyes. I wished you many happy returns of the day, and you came flying across the room and offered me your mouth to kiss. Or had you forgotten?'

There was a brief, loaded pause. Then, 'A moment of weakness,' she said. 'And a long time ago.'

'Ah,' he said softly. 'So you do remember?'

His glance brushed her mouth in overt reminiscence, and she felt her skin warm suddenly.

She said between her teeth, 'And before I discovered what a treacherous, money-grabbing sneak-thief you really were.'

'Ouch,' Chay said thoughtfully. 'Well, at least neither of us will be embarking on this liaison with any illusions about each other. That bodes well for our future, don't you think?'

'You don't want to know what I think. And, thanks to you, I don't have a future.'

'How do you reason that?'

She spread her hands, then realised there was an element of weakness in the gesture and let them fall to her sides instead.

'You say I could live my life, but that's rubbish. What kind of existence would I have, living here as your kept woman? Who the hell would want to know me under those circumstances?'

'Get real,' he said wearily. 'You're not some Victorian virgin, ruined by the wicked squire. What difference will it make to anyone?'

'It will make a hell of a difference to me,' she threw back at him.

'You didn't mind selling yourself to Piers Mendoza.' The casual contempt in his voice cut through the uneasy turmoil of emotion within her, bringing only swift, searing anger burning to the surface.

She said, 'Bastard,' and her hand came up to slap him across the face.

But his fingers caught her wrist, not gently, before the blow could reach its target.

'I see time hasn't soothed that temper of yours,' he remarked with a touch of grimness as he released her. 'Keep the fires damped down, Adrien, and don't trade on your gender. It won't work.'

She rubbed her wrist, staring at him with resentful eyes. 'I thought that was exactly what you wanted me to do.'

'Perhaps,' he said. 'But on my terms, not yours.'

'Which I'm not prepared to meet. So, buy someone else to share your bed. Because I'm telling you to go to hell,' she added fiercely.

He shrugged, unperturbed. 'That's your privilege, Adie. Go off—explore what other avenues you like. But don't be surprised if they all lead back to me.'

'I'm sure you'd like to think so,' she said. 'But if I have to degrade myself, I'd prefer to do it in my own way.'

'As you wish.' He paused. 'My offer stands, but it has a time limit. So, if you decide to change your mind, don't wait too long to tell me. I can be reached at the King's Arms.'

'Slumming at a hotel, Mr Haddon?' Adrien asked with contempt. 'I thought the new lord of the manor would have taken immediate possession.'

His glance went past her to the camp bed, standing forlorn and solitary beneath the window. His brows lifted mockingly. 'On that, darling? I prefer comfort—and room to manoeuvre.' He watched sudden colour invade her face, and laughed softly. 'I'll be waiting for your call.'

She lifted her chin. 'Don't hold your breath,' she advised scornfully, and walked past him, out of the room.

He said, 'You'll be back.'

'Never.'

'If only,' he continued, 'to collect this bag you've packed with such care.'

Adrien swung round, mortified, to find he was holding it, his mouth curved in amusement.

'Here,' he said. 'Catch.' And tossed it to her.

She clutched it inelegantly, caught off-balance in more ways than one, then gave him one last fulminating look before turning and heading for the stairs.

Walk, she told herself savagely, as she descended to the hall. Don't run. Don't let him think for one minute that he's got to you—even marginally.

But for all her bravado she was shaking when she got into the Jeep. She sat gripping the steering wheel until her hands ached, fighting for her self-control.

She thought, There must be something I can do. Oh, God, there just *has* to be…

Somehow she had to find a way out—a way of escape. But her immediate priority was to start the engine and get away. The last thing she wanted was to give Chay the satisfaction of finding her, sitting there as if she'd been turned to stone.

She drove home with immense care, using every atom of concentration she possessed. Not relaxing until she found herself turning the Jeep into the parking area at the rear of Listow Cottage. As she switched off the engine a small group of women came out of the workroom and walked past her, laughing and talking. When they spotted her, they gave a friendly wave.

And one day soon I'm going to have to tell them that they're out of work, Adrien thought, feeling sick as she lifted a hand in response. As she climbed out wearily, a football bounced towards her, with Smudge running behind it. His small, rather pale face was alive with excitement.

'Adie—Adie, guess what? We're getting a puppy. Mum says we can go and choose it this weekend.'

Adrien paused, forcing her cold lips into a semblance of a smile. 'Well—that's terrific,' she said, trying to ignore the sudden hollow feeling inside her.

Zelda had hesitantly asked a couple of weeks before if Adrien would mind her acquiring a dog.

'Smudge would really love one,' she'd said wistfully. 'And so would I. Dad would never let me have a pet of any kind when I was little.'

'I think it's a great idea,' Adrien had immediately approved. 'Have you any idea about breeds?'

Zelda laughed. 'I guess it'll be strictly a Heinz,' she'd said cheerfully. 'They've got a couple of litters at the animal sanctuary that'll be ready soon.'

I'll have to talk to Zelda straightaway, Adrien thought now, her heart sinking. Warn her that she may not be able to stay on here. That the whole place could be repossessed.

Zelda's door was standing ajar, so Adrien tapped and peeped round it, scenting the aroma of freshly ground coffee. Zelda was chopping vegetables at the table, but she looked up with a welcoming grin.

'Hi, stranger. I saw Smudge nail you. It is still all right about the puppy?'

She waved Adrien to a chair, set a couple of mugs on the table, and checked the percolator.

It was an incredibly warm and welcoming kitchen, Adrien thought, looking round. Zelda had chosen rich earth tones to complement the stone-flagged floor, and homely pine units. Smudge's paintings occupied places of honour on the terracotta walls, and several of them, Adrien saw with a pang, featured dogs.

Zelda had changed her own image too. The dark hair was now cut sleekly to her head, and she was wearing the black leggings and tunic that comprised her working gear. She looked sophisticated and relaxed, Adrien thought, a young woman in control of herself and her environment. But what would happen to her new-won confidence if she had to go back to the crowded family house and her father's unceasing complaints and strictures?

And how would Smudge cope? He'd been a quiet, almost withdrawn little boy when Adrien had first met him. A child who'd never had his own space. Who'd not been allowed to play in the garden in case he damaged the prize-winning begonias that his grandfather exhibited with such pride at the local flower show. A kid whose every word and action had been subject to restriction.

'Are you OK?' Zelda was staring at her. 'You're very quiet.'

Adrien smiled constrainedly. 'I've got a lot on my mind.'

'You certainly have.' Zelda grinned at her. 'The Grange to finish—a wedding to plan. In between it all, can you bend your mighty brain to the Westbrook Hotel? They've accepted my estimate for redoing all the bedroom curtains and covers, but now they're looking at a total revamp for the lounge and dining areas. Maisie Reed says she can't live with all those Regency stripes any longer. I said you'd go to see them.'

'Oh—fine.' Adrien rallied herself. 'When would they want the work doing?' If it was this autumn, she thought hopefully, and there was other work on hand too, she might be able to stave off the creditors for a while. Look for another lifeline.

'They're planning to close for January and February.' Zelda unwittingly dashed her hopes. 'Have a grand re-opening next Easter. It would be a good advertisement for us.'

'Yes,' Adrien said. 'Yes, it would.'

'Well, don't turn cartwheels.' Zelda brought the percolator to the table, with a jug of milk. 'There is a real world outside the Grange, and we need it.'

'I'm sorry.' Adrien steeled herself. 'It's just—there's a problem.'

Zelda gave her a long look, then poured the coffee carefully into the mugs. 'Major or minor?'

'Fairly major.' Adrien gulped down some of the black, fragrant brew to give her courage. 'The Grange has been sold—to a property developer called Chay Haddon.'

'Who plans to pull it down and build a theme park, I suppose.' Zelda reached a commiserating hand across the table. 'Love, I'm so sorry. I know all the time and effort you've put into the place. You must be gutted.' She paused, her eyes narrowing. 'When did Piers tell you?'

'He didn't.' Adrien withdrew her hand, clamping icy fingers round the mug instead. 'He left that to Chay Haddon himself—and the bank manager.'

Zelda said a short, sharp expletive. 'And where is Piers now?'

'In Brazil,' Adrien said tonelessly. 'Apparently on his honeymoon. I—I don't expect to hear from him.'

Zelda said, 'Oh, God,' and there was a brief, loaded silence. 'Honey, you won't believe me if I tell you that you're better off without him, but it's true. So who's this other bird?'

Adrien managed a shrug. 'Some rich Brazilian lady. I gather he's in financial trouble,' she added.

There was another pause, then Zelda said carefully, 'Is all this as bad as it sounds?'

'It's worse.' Adrien swallowed some more coffee. 'He—he cancelled his deposit to the payment account, and the bank's returned all the cheques. As my name's on the account, I have to carry the can. So—I'm broke.'

All Zelda's colour had faded, leaving a faint sprinkling of freckles across her nose.

She said, 'The new owner—isn't he liable? Couldn't he be...?'

Adrien bit her lip. 'No. And I've pulled out of the—the Grange project anyway. But he isn't going to pull it down. He plans to live there.' She forced a smile. 'On the whole I'd prefer demolition.'

'Chay Haddon,' Zelda said thoughtfully. 'The name's familiar.'

Adrien stared fiercely into her mug. 'He used to live at the Grange years ago,' she said. 'His mother was Mr Stretton's housekeeper.'

'I remember now,' Zelda said slowly. 'He used to come into town sometimes. Blond, sexy, but didn't say much.'

'His powers of speech seem to have expanded over the years.' Adrien's voice was wintry.

'But you must have known him quite well,' Zelda persisted, 'if he was at the Grange when you used to visit?'

'Yes,' Adrien said tightly. 'But we were never—friends.'

No, she thought, but for a while—when I was a little girl—he was my hero. And I worshipped him.

'Pity,' was Zelda's dry comment. 'It could have been handy.' She paused. 'So, what are we going to do?' She swallowed, her glance flickering round her clean but cluttered domain. 'Sell up and start again?'

'Oh, I hope it won't come to that,' Adrien said quickly, without any optimism at all. 'I'll find some way out. But I felt I ought to tell you before the rumours started flying.'

'Yes.' Zelda smiled with an effort. 'Thanks, babe.'

It was as if a light had been switched off inside her, Adrien thought wretchedly as she walked over to Listow Cottage and let herself in.

And Smudge had been even worse. He'd come dashing in, talking nineteen to the dozen about his puppy, and Zelda had put an arm round him and said gently that he might have to wait a little while longer.

Most children would have thrown some kind of tantrum, but Smudge had simply gone silent, his small face closed off and stoical, as if disappointment was nothing new to him.

It shouldn't be like that, Adrien thought angrily. He doesn't deserve it. And nor does Zelda.

She noticed without surprise that the answer-machine was winking furiously. The calls were from contractors who'd worked on the house, or suppliers, and without exception they wanted to know when they would be paid. And a few of them sounded frankly hostile.

She couldn't believe how rapidly she'd gone from being a valued colleague to a potential enemy.

She listed down their names and set them to one side.

There was no point in calling them back until she had a solution to offer, and at the moment there wasn't one.

Or nothing that she was prepared to contemplate, she amended stonily.

She tried to do some sums, but none of the numbers seemed to make sense, and the eventual total horrified her. It appeared that even if she was able to sell the business, plus the cottage and the outbuildings, including Zelda's conversion, there would still be a shortfall.

I'm ruined, she thought blankly. We all are. And it's Chay Haddon's fault. Forcing his way back into our lives. Using his money like a sledgehammer to get what he wants.

Shivering, she wrapped her arms protectively round her body.

Piers, she thought with anguish. Why didn't you tell me that you were in financial trouble? I could have stopped work on the house. Why didn't you warn me...?

But it wasn't simply the money, a small, cold voice in her head reminded her. There was also the personal betrayal of the affair in Portugal, and she couldn't reasonably blame Chay for that, although she wished she could.

But it had been entirely Piers's own decision to dump her and run. To leave her abandoned and practically destitute while he married someone else without even a word...

Up to that moment she seemed to have been numbed by disbelief. Now, pain came over her like a black wave, swamping coherent thought, constricting her throat and dragging her mouth into a rictus of grief. She heard herself moan, and found, suddenly, that she was free-falling into some dark chasm of hurt and fear.

She groped her way to a chair by the table, put her head down on the smooth wooden surface, and began to weep without restraint, her whole body convulsed by the sobs that tore through her, so that she ached with the force of them.

When, at last, they began to subside, she stayed where she was, her face buried in her folded arms, an occasional shiver curling down her spine. She felt utterly drained, and when she got to her feet her legs were shaky.

Not altogether surprising, she reminded herself, as she'd had nothing to eat since breakfast, and those two slices of toast now seemed to belong to another lifetime.

She felt empty, but at the same time the thought of food was repulsive. She felt hot and disorientated, and her bout of weeping had left an odd metallic taste in her mouth. She filled the kettle and set it to boil, then realised she didn't really want tea or coffee either.

I need something stronger, she thought, and headed down to the cellar, emerging a few minutes later with a bottle of white burgundy.

She found the corkscrew and took a crystal glass from the wall cupboard in the dining room, then carried them all into the sitting room.

It was showing signs of her absence. There was a film of dust on the polished surfaces, and a vase of dead flowers on the table below the window.

She sat down in one of the big chairs that flanked the fireplace, and leaned back against the cushions.

Outside, the light was fading rapidly, and there was a faint chill in the air which spoke of autumn. *The days are drawing in.* That was what people said, and they hung heavier curtains at their windows, and lit fires in the evening, and started to make plans for Christmas. All the usual, normal things.

Only this year it would not happen. Not for her, or Zelda.

In the course of one day her life had changed for ever. All its certainties gone.

By Christmas, heaven only knows where we'll all be,

she thought bleakly, and drank some wine. Its crisp, cold fruitiness filled her mouth and caressed her dry, aching throat, and she savoured it gratefully.

There were tall shelves in the recesses beside the fireplace which had been filled with books and ornaments. There was a radio just beside her, and she switched it on, turning the dial until she found a station playing classical music.

The sound filled the room, haunting and wistful—an orchestral version of Debussy's 'Girl with the Flaxen Hair'.

Adrien closed her eyes as the music washed over her, seeing the girl, her blonde hair shining in the sunlight, walking through a meadow, dreaming, perhaps, of her wedding, as she made her way back to some solid French farmhouse. Her life, she thought, would be safe, and secure, and full of hope.

Whereas I—I have no hope at all. I'm going to lose everything I've worked for. Every dream I ever had.

Maybe I should change my hair to blonde, she thought with bitter self-mockery. They say blondes have more fun.

She drank some more wine, and refilled her glass.

So much of her future had been wrapped up in Piers it seemed impossible that he was no longer part of her life. She'd created this image of their relationship in her mind, and invested all her emotional energy in it.

He dazzled me, she thought, from the first moment I saw him, even though I was only a child. He was so glamorous, and so different. And, after Chay let me down, he made me trust him.

And he knew it. My God, when he came back, I must have been a sitting duck. I just accepted everything he told me—went along with his schemes. Walked blindly into his trap.

But now that he'd gone she felt strangely numb—hollow—as if nothing mattered any longer, she thought, almost dreamily. As if every bit of emotion had been drained out of her, leaving only a shell. As if the girl she had been simply didn't exist any more.

She drank again, feeling the wine spreading warmth through her chilled veins. Seeing the difficulties surrounding her with a new clarity.

Because, she realised with cool finality, she didn't have to be a loser. She had a choice. Not an enviable one, but a serious option.

Piers didn't want her, but there was another man who did. All she had to do was agree to his terms and her problems would be solved. Well—most of them, anyway, she amended, wincing.

He'd offered her a business arrangement, so she didn't have to pretend to be in love with him—or even to want him. He could have the shell—the empty husk she'd become. Because there was nothing else.

She emptied her glass, staring into space. She would loan herself to him for a set time—a finite term. That was the only way she'd be able to bear it: if she could remind herself each day—and each night—that the situation was temporary. If she could know for certain that she would eventually be free of him, and that he would have no further claim on her.

She shivered violently. It all sounded so—cold-blooded. Yet that was the deal he'd suggested, and that was the bargain she'd made. No more and no less.

That way the business would be safe, and so would this house. And Zelda and Smudge would be secure too.

So many good reasons for degrading herself. For offering herself for sale. For going against every principle she possessed.

But I can't afford principles, she reminded herself harshly, refilling her glass again. I have to be pragmatic. Do the expedient thing.

And I must do it now. While I still have the courage.

She got up so quickly that her head swam, and made her way to the telephone, dialling the King's Arms hotel. Not giving herself time to think—to change her mind, or clutch at sanity.

A girl answered, briskly polite. 'King's Arms—Reception. How may I help you?'

Adrien cleared her throat. 'You have a Mr Haddon staying with you. May I speak to him, please?'

'I'm sorry, madam, Mr Haddon isn't here at the moment, although we're expecting him to return for dinner. May I take a message?'

Yes, thought Adrien, feeling a crazy giggle trying to escape. Tell him I'll sleep with him if he pays all the debts on the Grange.

Aloud, she said, rather more sedately, 'Will you tell him that Miss Lander called, please?'

'Of course, madam. Is he expecting to hear from you?'

There was a pause, then, 'Yes,' Adrien said with difficulty. 'Yes, I—I rather think he is.'

And gently she replaced the receiver.

She lifted her head and stared at herself in the wall mirror above the telephone table. Her face was white, except for a trace of hectic colour on her cheekbones, and her eyes were blurred with weeping.

'Some bargain,' she derided herself shakily. 'But I've done it now—and I can't afford to turn back. The stakes are too high.'

She lifted her glass in a parody of a toast.

'To the future,' she said huskily. And drank.

CHAPTER FOUR

ADRIEN had picked up the splinter on her climb to the tree-house. The sliver of wood was now embedded firmly in her knee, with dark drops of blood welling up around it.

'Let me have a look.' Chay sat her down on his rolled up sleeping bag and scrutinised the damage with faint impatience. 'I can get it out,' he said, at last. 'But it's going to hurt. Can you keep very still while I do it?'

She nodded mutely, biting her lip hard, because it was already hurting, but reluctant to let him see. He might decide she was a nuisance, and never let her come up to the treehouse again. Never let her use the field glasses to watch birds and rabbits and squirrels, or give her a sheet from his sketching block and show her how to draw a tree or a flower.

He opened the old biscuit tin she thought of as his treasure box. It held a compass, a magnifying glass, pens and pencils, a wonderful knife, with all sorts of blades that she wasn't allowed to touch, and a pair of tweezers.

He was quick and deft, but when he'd finished her eyes were filled with tears although she hadn't made a sound.

He looked up at her, and his thin face softened. 'You were very brave,' he said, and her lips trembled into a smile. 'But it really needs bathing, and maybe a tetanus shot.' He produced a clean handkerchief from the pocket of his jeans and tied it round the little wound. 'You'd better go home and let your mother have a look at it.'

He saw her droop with disappointment, and stood up briskly. 'And don't look as if you're being punished,' he cautioned sternly. 'The house will still be here tomorrow.

And so will I.' And he touched her cheek gently and fleetingly with his finger…

'My God,' Adrien whispered, shooting bolt-upright in her chair, her heart thumping. 'I must have been dreaming.'

But was it a dream? she wondered uneasily, as she stared round the sitting room. Or a long-buried memory that suddenly, and for no good reason, had come swimming to the surface of her consciousness?

And 'swimming' was the appropriate word, she thought, shaking her head. She felt positively fuzzy.

Slowly, she pulled up the hem of her skirt, and looked down at the tiny silver scar on her knee. It had been there so long—so much a part of her physical make-up—that she never really registered it any more. Or hadn't done so. Until now, when she'd suddenly remembered how she'd acquired it.

But I know why I forgot, she thought slowly. Because the next time I went to the Grange Piers was there—and everything changed. The treehouse stopped being a sanctuary and became a nightmare. And Chay wasn't my hero or my friend any more, but my enemy.

Besides, a splinter in the knee was nothing to the other wounds she'd suffered at Chay's hands, then and afterwards. The scarring was hidden, internal, but still potent, she realised bitterly.

And he hadn't finished with her yet.

Shivering, she rose to her feet, and paused, aware that she felt hollow and still faintly dizzy. While she'd been dozing, or whatever, it had got dark. And cold too. Perhaps she was catching a chill, and that was why she felt so shaky.

Moving gingerly, she lit the lamps, and had started towards the window to draw the curtains when the brisk sound of the doorbell halted her in her tracks.

She stood for a moment, aware that her mouth was suddenly dry and her pulses drumming. Also that she was swaying slightly where she stood. And that her head seemed stuffed with feathers.

If she hadn't switched on the damned lights she could have pretended she wasn't there. As it was, she might as well have been standing in a goldfish bowl.

Reluctantly, she felt her way into the hall, and opened the door, gasping as a blast of cool air hit her.

'Good evening,' Chay said. 'I got your message. May I come in?'

'What do you want?' She wrapped her arms defensively round her body.

'I think that's really my question. You called me—remember?'

'Yesh,' she said, and swallowed. 'Er—yes, I did.' She propped herself against the doorframe. 'You certainly don't waste any time.'

He gave her a searching look. 'Not very welcoming, darling. Have you had a change of heart?'

In spite of her sense of fragility, Adrien sent back a challenging stare. 'No,' she said. 'I—I rang because I've decided to accept your offer.'

'I thought you would,' he murmured.

She glared at him, hating him. 'And the victor's here to claim his shpoils.'

His smile was ironic. 'I think it's pronounced "spoils". And also that it's a little early to claim total victory.' He gave her a moment to digest this. Then, 'Do you plan to conduct this entire interview standing on the doorstep?'

Adrien gave him a mutinous glare. 'It's thish way.' She started towards the sitting room, pausing to touch base with the wall and the hall table as she went.

Chay caught up with her and took her arm. 'Let me help.' But she pulled away.

'Leave me alone. I can walk round my own housh.' She frowned, drew a breath, and enunciated 'house' with great clarity.

She gestured towards the wine bottle. 'Would you like a glass of wine?' Pleased with herself, she repeated, 'A glass of wine?' She picked up the bottle and held it up to the light. 'Oh,' she said. 'There's none left.'

'Now, why does that not surprise me?' Chay gave her another long look. 'When did you last eat?'

She gave the matter frowning consideration. 'I don't remember. And what hash it to do with you, anyway?'

'Just kindly concern for your well-being, Adie.'

'Kindly concern?' Adrien repeated. 'Isn't that a little out of character?'

He laughed. 'Prompted entirely by self-interest, darling, I assure you. After all, I've no wish for you to die of malnutrition before we've had the chance to consummate our bargain.' He paused. 'Tell me, were you in this condition when you called the hotel?'

She said with dignity, 'I don't know what you're talking about. I don't have a condition.'

'No?' He looked amused. 'Now, I'd have said you'd been drowning your sorrows, and to some measure.'

'Well, I'm not likely to be shelebrating.' She frowned. 'I mean...'

'It's all right,' he said. 'I get the idea. I think I'll continue the funereal theme with some black coffee. I presume the kitchen's through here?'

Adrien followed, watching with a kind of mute indignation as he deftly filled the kettle, and set it to boil, then found the coffee jar and two beakers.

She said freezingly, 'Make yourself at home.'

'Thanks.' He remained calmly unfrozen. Even slanted a smile at her.

'What exactly are you doing here?' Adrien demanded.

'I felt we'd better sort a few important details. When you're sober enough to deal with them, that is.'

'I'm not drunk,' she denied with emphasis.

'No,' he said soothingly. 'Just a little fuzzy round the edges. And I'd really prefer you to be thinking straight.'

She drew a stormy breath. 'And your wishes, of course, are paramount.'

He said softly, 'So you've come to terms with that already. Excellent. I thought you'd find it far more of a hurdle.'

'Actually, I was being—' She considered 'sarcastic' then opted for safety with 'ironic'.

'I'd never have guessed.' He poured boiling water on to granules, and handed her a beaker. 'Try this. Have you got any eggs?'

'No,' she said blandly. 'The cupboard is bare. Don't forget, I've been staying at the Grange.'

'How could I forget?' Chay said softly. 'It's fragrant with your presence.' He shrugged. 'But it doesn't matter about the food. I'll ring that French place in Market Street and get them to send us something.'

'If you mean Ma Maison,' Adrien said sharply, 'they don't do takeaway.'

He smiled at her. 'Then I'll just have to talk them round.'

The coffee was strong and scalding, and one mouthful cleared her head and steadied her tongue. The second put new heart into her. She lifted her chin. 'Has it occurred to you that I might not want to have dinner with you?'

'Yes,' he said. 'But I dismissed the idea. We have to take that first step together some time, and it might as well be sooner rather than later.'

She put the beaker down on the worktop. She said carefully, 'When you say "first step"…?'

'I mean dinner,' he said. 'Just that. Only that. What, in other circumstances, might be termed a date.'

Adrien raised her eyebrows. 'Except that I would never go on a date with you. Under any circumstances.'

'Then I'm glad I never asked you.' He grinned at her. 'Imagine the dent to my pride.'

She said with sudden fierceness, 'And the role you have planned for me? The fact that you're—buying me, when you know I'm in love with someone else? Do you have pride in that?'

'Upon which I'm supposed to hang my head in shame and slink back into the night?' Chay's smile widened. 'Nice try, darling.'

'Don't you have any scruples?'

He gave a negligent shrug. 'I've managed pretty well without them up to now. And I didn't think they were a priority with you, either, if your ex-boyfriend is anything to go by.'

'Don't you dare criticise Piers,' she said thickly. 'At least he's not a rapist.'

'And nor am I,' he said softly. 'As I shall have exquisite pleasure in demonstrating to you before too long.' He paused, to allow his words to be assimilated. 'And now I'll order us some food. I hear their lemon chicken is good.'

'I don't want any bloody chicken.'

'You'd prefer the cassoulet?'

'No.' Her voice rose. 'Don't you care that I still love Piers?'

'I admit it doesn't say much for your critical faculties,' he said. 'But look on it as an illness. Something childish and unpleasant, like measles. You'll get over it.'

'Perhaps I don't want to,' she hurled back recklessly.

He said quietly, 'Now you're being ridiculous. You were always blinkered where he was concerned, but that's carrying things too far.' He paused. 'However, if that's really how you feel, why did you call me?'

'Self-interest,' she said. 'I hear there's a lot of it about.

Besides, you didn't leave me much choice.' She squared her shoulders defensively. 'I decided I wasn't prepared to lose everything I've worked for, particularly when there are other people involved who'd go down with me, and you were the only person to offer a solution. But that doesn't mean I have to like it.'

'"Like" is a pallid word,' he said musingly. 'I prefer—"enjoy".' He smiled at her. 'As you will.'

'Never.' Her voice was passionate. 'Never in this world.'

He sent her a meditative look. 'I strongly advise you to try. You'll find it much easier that way.' He paused again. 'Anyway,' he added softly, 'I don't think you know what you like.'

Her heart missed a beat. 'What,' she said 'is that supposed to mean?'

'I'm sure you can work it out.' His tone was dry. 'Now, get your coat. I've decided that we'll eat at the restaurant instead.'

'I don't want to go out,' she said defiantly.

'You'll find it safer.' The winter eyes swept her, stripping her naked with one devastating glance. 'The urge to take you to bed and teach you several much needed lessons is becoming almost overwhelming.' He watched the rush of hot colour into her face and nodded. 'Besides, it's good policy for us to be seen in public together,' he went on. 'It may stop your creditors beating the door down.'

Adrien bit her lip. 'Yes,' she said unevenly, angry to find she was trembling. 'Yes, I—I can see that.'

The room seemed suddenly to have shrunk to claustrophobic proportions, making it difficult for her to breathe properly.

She took another gulp of coffee, steadying herself.

She said, 'Does it—have to be Ma Maison?'

'You don't like it there?'

'I—used to go there a lot.'

He sighed. 'With Piers?'

'Naturally.'

'And now you're going with me,' he said. 'And soon that will seem equally natural.'

'There's an Italian place in the Square...'

'Adie,' he said. 'I'm not going to waste time avoiding places you might have visited with your ex-lover. Life is too short. Now, fetch your jacket.'

She said bitterly. 'Yes, my lord. To hear is to obey.'

He laughed. 'Now you're getting the idea. And hurry, please. It's a long time since I ate, too.'

She glanced down at her creased blouse and rumpled skirt. 'I really should change.' She made it tentative.

'Fine.' His tone was equable. 'I'll wait for you here.'

She walked past him, across the hall to the stairs, turning on the bottom step and posing, hand on hip, her whole body a deliberate challenge.

'You mean you're not planning to watch?' She mimicked astonishment, her eyes flashing contempt.

'Why, yes,' he said. 'But only when I choose to do so. I'm setting the scenario here, darling. Not you. Try and remember that.' He paused. 'So, don't keep me waiting or make me fetch you, because you could seriously regret it.'

'Don't worry,' Adrien threw over her shoulder. 'I already have all the regrets I can handle.'

'I shouldn't count on that,' Chay sent grimly after her.

Reaching her bedroom, Adrien was sorely tempted to lock the door, but she knew it would be a waste of time. Chay's body might be lean, but it was strong and muscular. Any physical contest between them he would win effortlessly, even if there was an elderly door in the way.

She looked at herself in the mirror, swallowing convulsively as she saw the pale face and hunted eyes.

Her decision to change her clothes had been purely an excuse—a temporary escape route from the ordeal of confrontation. She'd begun to feel stifled downstairs—totally trapped. Yet she had no one but herself to blame.

Finding herself alone with Chay had brought the true implications of her decision forcibly home to her. So far he had barely laid a hand on her, but all too soon that would change. And she would have to accept it.

Although something warned her that Chay would not settle for mere acceptance. She had agreed, after all, to be his mistress—his partner in passion. Which was almost funny under the circumstances, except that she didn't feel like laughing.

And if Chay came upstairs and found her, in her underwear, staring into space, she might have even less to be amused about, she thought drearily, treading across to the wardrobe.

Most of her things were working gear. The few play clothes she possessed she'd bought for Piers, loving to dress up for him and hear his voice murmur in approval.

None of them seemed—appropriate for this occasion. Except for one outfit, which she'd bought but never worn. She'd been saving it for Piers's next visit, she realised, wincing.

She took it out and surveyed it. It was a top and skirt in silvery grey voile, overlaid with a pattern in black. The filmy skirt was knee-length, and fluted at the hem, and the top had tiny cap sleeves and a deep vee neck. Too deep for the workaday bra she was wearing, she decided, rooting through her drawer for the only one she possessed with sufficient plunge. But it wasn't there, and she thought, To hell with it, and slid the top over her head.

It was a good choice, she decided, the lines discreetly fluid, the skirt flowing round her slim body. She used blusher and eyeshadow swiftly and deftly, then ran a brush through her hair, tying it at the nape of her neck with a black silk scarf. She thrust her feet into low-heeled black kid shoes, grabbed up a matching purse and a black silk-knit jacket.

When she got downstairs, Chay was standing in the sitting room doorway, leaning one shoulder against its frame.

'I was just starting to get impatient,' he commented, his brows lifting as he surveyed her. 'Now I'm impressed.'

'Don't be,' Adrien said brusquely. 'I haven't dressed for you. I'm certain that tongues will already be wagging about my financial problems. So, whatever the outcome of tonight's negotiations, I don't intend to look like a loser.'

'You doubt that our deal will be concluded to our—mutual satisfaction?' The mockery in his tone scratched across her nerve-endings.

'It takes two to make a bargain,' she returned coolly. 'And I have certain stipulations of my own.'

'I'm sure you have,' he murmured, straightening. 'Shall we go?'

Ma Maison wasn't very large, but the intimate ambience and the quality of its food ensured that it was always busy.

Adrien had secretly hoped that they'd be politely but regretfully turned away. It would be good, she thought vengefully, to see Chay thwarted, even in such a minor way. But instead they were met with smiles and shown to a secluded corner table, sheltered from the rest of the room by a large weeping fig tree.

There was also an ice bucket, containing a bottle of Moët et Chandon and two champagne flutes.

Adrien took her seat and looked at her companion across the table. She said, tight-lipped, 'When did you actually make this reservation?'

'Not long after you made your outraged departure from the Grange. I'm glad I judged the situation correctly,' he added silkily.

She said between her teeth, 'My God, you're sure of yourself.'

'No,' he said. 'Just good at assessing the variables. That's why I've prospered, whilst Piers is in Brazil with a woman who'll soon tire of him, even though she is pregnant.'

She looked down at the immaculate white cloth. 'I don't want to hear about that.'

'Rubbish,' Chay said briskly. 'You're only sorry I haven't got photographs. Now you can tell me I'm totally insensitive—or are you still slurring your words?'

Adrien stared at him. She said, 'You bastard.'

'Well, that was clear enough.' The grey eyes glinted at her. 'But smile when you say it. We're being watched.' He handed her a menu. 'And don't tell me you're not hungry,' he added. 'You need something to soak up that bottle of wine.'

'Thank you,' Adrien said, putting down the menu without a glance. 'I'll have fillet steak and a green salad.'

'Just as you wish,' he said equably. 'It's your loss, not mine. But, as you've come here to negotiate, a degree of co-operation might serve you better.'

There was a silence, then Adrien, biting her lip, reached for the menu.

He was right about them being the centre of attention, she realised, sheltering behind the dark brown leather covers. Although, if she was honest, it was Chay who was attracting the sideways glances and murmured comments, not herself. Because it was the other women in the restaurant who were looking, their eyes lingering and speculative, and, in some cases, envious.

If only they knew, she thought bitterly.

And yet—and yet—if she was seeing him for the first time—encountering him as a stranger, with no past or hidden agenda—what would she think?

He had a powerful physical presence, she admitted unwillingly. The silent, rather shy boy had been left behind
long ago. And the cool eyes now held a world of experience
in their mocking gaze.

Perhaps this was what those other women sensed. He
might be wealthy, but he would never need money as an
aphrodisiac because he already possessed a potent sexual
charisma.

She might resent it, but she had to be aware of it. And
she had to fear it, she thought, swallowing.

'Have you decided?'

She said huskily, 'It—it seems so.' And was glad that
the menu was hiding her from him, so that he could not
see her eyes.

Food was a kind of salvation. A note of normality in a
reeling world. In the end they both chose the terrine, after
which she had the lemon chicken while Chay opted for the
cassoulet. She even drank some of the champagne when it
was poured into her glass, and listened to Chay making
light, amusing conversation with a smile that felt as if she'd
nailed it there.

Several people came across to the table to greet her—a
couple of former clients and the rest barest acquaintances—
all of them wanting to be introduced to Chay.

Adrien, face and voice expressionless, explained that he
was the new owner of the Grange, and saw interest mount.

Wait until they find I've moved in there, she thought
wearily. They'll have a field-day.

She supposed she could only be thankful that her en-
gagement to Piers had never been made official—or public.
Local people had speculated, naturally, but no one, apart
from Zelda, had known that Piers had indeed asked her to
marry him.

'I want to do it in style,' he'd told her. 'Throw an enormous house-warming party and invite the whole county. Until then let's keep them guessing.'

Adrien had chafed at the restriction, but now she was thankful. The rumours already flying about her financial status were bad enough, but they'd be dispelled soon by even more fascinating gossip. Somehow to have it known she'd been tricked and abandoned—and to be pitied or laughed at—would have been infinitely worse.

Whereas here she was, dining out with a new man, seemingly without a care in the world. So let them think and say what they liked. Now and for ever.

The main course was served, the wine poured, and the waiter left them alone.

'So,' Chay said softly. 'Shall we talk business?'

'Perhaps we should.' Adrien chewed a piece of her delectable chicken as if it was the sole of an old boot, and swallowed it with difficulty. 'From what you said this afternoon, you're prepared to pay the debts I've incurred over the Grange, and allow the remaining work to be finished, if I—make myself available to you. Is that right?'

'Yes.' The candlelight made his eyes glitter oddly.

She concentrated on cutting another morsel of chicken. 'So—how long would this—arrangement last?'

'I beg your pardon?' His voice was quiet.

She gestured with her fork. 'Weeks—months—a year? How long before you'd consider the debt paid and let me go?'

'That's difficult to assess,' he said after a pause. 'I'd expect my money's worth.'

She stared rigidly at her plate. 'Yes.'

'Have you worked out how much cash you need.'

'Approximately,' she said huskily, and named the figure. It sounded outrageous—and maybe it would be. Perhaps, even at this late stage, he'd decide she wasn't worth it after all.

But he nodded, apparently unfazed. 'You'd better let me have an exact rundown of all the people you owe, and the amounts. I'll arrange for my PA to have the money transferred to the account you've been using.'

'When?' Adrien asked baldly.

He said softly, 'When you've fulfilled your part of the bargain, Adrien—and to my complete satisfaction.' He smiled at her. 'So the timing is entirely down to you.'

'That's not fair.' Her voice sounded stifled. 'I can't guarantee to—be what you want—to please you.'

'Come now, darling,' he said mockingly. 'Don't tell me that the fire in that beautiful hair of yours is all bad temper. I'm sure Piers didn't think so.'

Her back stiffened. 'But that's totally different. I—I loved Piers.'

'And you hate me. Is that what you're trying to say?'

She said curtly, 'You can hardly blame me.'

His mouth twisted. 'Love and hate, Adie. Opposite sides of the same coin. And in bed, believe me, the distinction can become very blurred.' He paused. 'But I've been patient for a long time. I can wait a while longer for you to accept the situation.'

'A year,' she said. 'Whatever happens, you have to let me go after a year. That has to be my absolute limit. Do you agree?'

He shrugged a shoulder. 'If that's what you want. But has it occurred to you, Adie, that a year might be too long? That six months might be a more realistic target? After all, I get bored very easily,' he added softly. 'So your ordeal may be over sooner than you think.'

She said hoarsely, 'Six hours—six minutes—would be too much for me. And I want my own room—my own space. Somewhere that I can pretend none of this is happening.'

'You can have a whole suite,' he said. 'But you occupy

it while I'm not there. When I'm staying at the Grange you share my life and my bed. Understood?'

Mutely, she nodded.

'Then it's all settled. Now eat some of your chicken before it's cold.'

She said, very distinctly, 'Another mouthful would choke me.'

He grinned. 'You wish.'

She said slowly, 'How do you know that I won't simply empty the account and vanish?'

'I don't,' he said. 'I'm counting on your regard for your colleagues and creditors outweighing your resentment of me. They'd have to bear the brunt if you went, and I know you don't want that.'

'No,' she said. 'Damn you.'

'If ever I thought I was irresistible, tonight would be one hell of an eye-opener,' he commented sardonically. Then his voice became businesslike again. 'My furniture will be arriving during the week. I'd like you to supervise the unloading and arrangement, and complete the outstanding work on the house. There isn't that much left to do.'

'You mentioned staff...'

'My present housekeeper will be joining me. I'd like you to engage local cleaners, and contractors to handle the gardening. If you have a problem, talk to my PA. Her name's Sally Parfitt, and you can reach her here.' He handed a Haddon Developments business card across to her.

'I shall be in Brussels until the end of the week,' he added. 'But I'll be coming down to the Grange on Friday evening.' He paused. 'And I expect to find you there, Adie. Warm and welcoming. No excuses.'

She said tonelessly, 'I'll—be there. I've said so.'

'I'd prefer a little more conviction—and commitment,' he said silkily. 'But I can wait. And now shall we shake hands on our bargain—for the sake of our audience?'

She stared down at the table as his fingers closed round hers, only to glance up, startled, as he turned her hand over and bent his head to drop a kiss on to its palm.

For one searing moment she felt the flicker of his tongue against her soft skin, and her body jerked in shock at the brief intimacy of the contact.

He straightened, his eyes glinting as they took a leisurely toll of her, lingering on her parted lips and the hurried swell of her breasts.

'You taste like Paradise,' he told her softly. 'Friday just can't come soon enough.'

'For you.' The words were barely audible. 'But not for me.'

She pushed back her chair, and got to her feet, collecting her jacket and bag.

She said, clearly and calmly, 'Goodnight, Mr Haddon. And—thank you. I—look forward to working with you. Have a pleasant trip.'

And with a smile that acknowledged the other diners, Adrien, her head held high, walked to the door and out into the chill of the night.

CHAPTER FIVE

SHE was breathless when she reached the cottage, almost flinging herself through the front door. She snapped on the central lamp in the hall, then found herself running from room to room, pressing light switches with feverish energy until the whole ground floor was lit up like a Christmas tree.

Anything—*anything*—to dispel the darkness that seemed to be closing around her. The darkness that Chay Haddon had brought.

And that other inexplicable darkness inside her that had responded to the brush of his mouth on her flesh.

Adrien shivered, wrapping her arms round her body, her throat tightening convulsively.

He took me by surprise, she thought defensively. That's all it was. I was startled. In future I shall be on my guard. And stone-cold sober. All that wine—and then champagne. That was the problem.

She nodded fiercely as she started towards the kitchen. More black coffee was what she needed. And what did it matter if it kept her awake? After the events of the past twenty-four hours she was unlikely to sleep anyway.

She'd just filled the kettle and set it to boil when the tap came at the back door.

Zelda must have seen all the lights go on and popped across to check that she was all right. Only Adrien wasn't sure she wanted to talk right now. She was afraid that she might say too much—alert her partner to what she was planning. Because, no matter what the consequences might be, Zelda would forbid her to do it. She knew that.

She hastily put the coffee jar away and took down the packet of herbal teas instead. She'd claim she was tired, and making a bedtime drink. Send Zelda away reassured.

Bracing herself, she opened the door and found herself staring up at Chay Haddon's unsmiling face.

'What are you doing here?' Her voice sounded unnaturally husky.

'Don't play games.' He stepped into the kitchen, kicking the door shut behind him. 'It was a terrific exit, Adie, but you didn't fool anyone, least of all me. I can't wait until Friday, and neither, I suspect from your reaction, can you.'

'Get out of here,' she said, her throat tightening. 'Get out of my house.'

He shook his head. 'You don't mean that, and you know it. Because you're as curious as I am—wondering how it'll be between us.'

'No,' she said. And again, desperately, 'No—we had an agreement...'

'It's a dangerous world out there,' he said. 'And a lot can happen in a week. I might not come back. You might run after all. And I need to know, Adie. I need to know how long you'll maintain those stony defences of yours once your clothes are off. How your body's going to feel against mine—under mine. Whether your mouth will be honey and musk—just as I've always dreamed.'

He took a step towards her and she backed away, lifting her hands in front of her in a futile effort to ward him off.

'Please...'

'Why not?' His brows lifted.

'It's too soon,' she said hoarsely. 'I—I'm not ready.'

He shrugged. 'Sooner—later. What real difference does it make? You gave your word, Adie. Are you reneging on your promise.'

'No.' Adrien bit her lip. 'But by Friday I'll have had a chance to think it all through. To prepare myself.'

Chay shook his head. He said softly, 'I disagree. I say it's time you stopped thinking—and started feeling instead.'

He took another step forward, and she retreated again, only to find herself blocked by the work surface behind her.

'Poor Adie,' he said. 'Nowhere left to run.' He was close to her now, but still not touching. She could almost feel the warmth of his skin. Sense the tautness of his muscular body. She stared up at him, aware that her legs were shaking.

And he looked back at her, his mouth twisting in something that was not quite a smile.

He said quietly, 'Close your eyes, darling.'

'Why should I?' Her voice sounded thick.

'Because it's the first barrier, and I want it removed.'

He made it sound totally reasonable, and after a pause she obeyed, feeling an enervating weakness spreading through her body as the chilling inevitability of it all began to invade her conscious mind.

He was going to kiss her, she thought. And that was not new. She'd briefly known the touch of his mouth on hers already.

But what would follow was totally outside her experience, and she could feel panic closing her throat.

His arm went round her, drawing her forward, gently but quite inexorably, and she swallowed, golden lights dancing behind her closed eyelids and she waited for his lips to take hers.

Instead, she was aware of his fingertips, light as gossamer, on her hair as he stroked it back from her face, before moving slowly over her temple and down to her cheekbone. The brush of his fingers followed the shape of her face, then discovered the faint hollow below her ear, where they lingered, tracing a gentle, tantalising spiral. That was, she realised, shocked, almost enjoyable.

As enjoyable, in fact, as the delicate movement of his other hand against her spine, making the silk of her top shiver against her skin.

A faint, insidious excitement was sending its first tendrils through her being, drying her mouth and sending her pulse-beat ragged.

Her voice didn't sound as if it belonged to her. 'Why are you doing this—please...?'

'Hush.' His mouth just touched her parted lips in a caress so fleeting she might have imagined it. 'You don't look. You don't speak. Speech is the second barrier.'

She could just capture a trace of the cologne he wore—expensive, but elusive. Seductive enough to tempt her to put her face against his tanned skin and breathe it deeply.

But she couldn't afford any more temptation, she realised breathlessly. Not while she stood, blind and silent in his arms, her whole body tingling with awareness of those tiny patterns his fingers were drawing on her flesh. And not just awareness. Arousal.

A slow, sensuous warmth was spreading through her veins, drugging her, blotting out all sensation but the sub-tlety of his caresses.

And just as she thought that she couldn't bear any more, that she'd have to beg him to stop, his hand moved down-wards, skimming the slender line of her neck and throat, to the smooth angle of her shoulder. Where he paused.

A small sound rose in her throat, to be instantly stifled, and in return she thought she heard him whisper, 'Yes.'

His fingers slid beneath the neckline of her top, pushing aside the flimsy edge as he began to explore the delicate line of her collarbone, so minutely that he might have been committing it to memory.

Adrien was dimly aware that her stance had changed. That she was no longer rigid within his encircling arm but leaning back, her body gently slackening, allowing him to support her. And that under the silky top her breasts were tautening in anticipation of the moment that would come when he... Ah, dear God, the moment that was here—now.

Her breasts seemed to blossom and flower at his touch, the nipples erect and eager for the flutter of his fingers against their hardening peaks.

Her back arched in sensuous joy and demand, all thought of resistance finally ebbing away. She felt the edge of the wooden worktop pressing against her back as his other hand moved slowly down in its turn, smoothing its way over the curve of her flank and lingering over the slender pliancy of her thigh. Leaving her on some knife-edge of bewilderment and need, her body hot and fluid in anticipation of his touch.

Her nipples were aching, on fire with pleasure. She wanted him to kiss them—longed to experience the balm of his tongue.

Her thighs had already parted—inviting his exploration—pleading with him to discover this intense molten desire for him in a demand more potent for being silent.

Her breathing was in tense abeyance, her lower lip caught between her teeth in an attempt to balance the pain of this unlooked for yearning.

And then, like the lash of a whip across her senses, it was over. Chay released her, straightening her clothing in one practised movement.

'I think you have a visitor.' His voice was cool, even expressionless, as if he was some stranger with whom she'd been exchanging thoughts on the weather, Adrien thought dazedly.

Then, instantly, she heard Zelda's voice outside the back door, calling, 'Adrien—are you there! Are you all right?'

By the time she'd opened the door and walked in Chay was on the other side of the kitchen, attending to the kettle which had come unnoticed to the boil.

'Oh.' Zelda checked in obvious embarrassment when she saw him. 'I'm sorry. I saw all the lights come on and wondered… I didn't realise…'

'Everything's fine.' His smile was relaxed, charming. As if she was the one person in the world he'd wanted to see, and at that particular moment, Adrien thought with a silent gasp of outrage. 'I was on the point of leaving, anyway,' he added, adding fuel to the flames. 'I just had—a few final details to settle with Miss Lander.'

'Well, if you're sure,' Zelda began doubtfully.

'Totally.' He nodded for emphasis, then turned to Adrien, his expression cool—even impersonal. 'I think that little discussion has made things much clearer, don't you? I look forward to continuing our dialogue next Friday. Please don't move,' he added quickly, as she took a half-step forward, her lips parting indignantly. 'I'll see myself out.'

He favoured them both with another swift smile, and was gone.

'Well,' Zelda said, with a wealth of meaning. 'So, what was that all about?'

'I don't know what you mean,' Adrien said evasively, wondering if she could walk across the kitchen without her legs collapsing under her. Her body, subjected to the sexual equivalent of cold turkey treatment, had gone into shock.

Zelda gave her an old-fashioned look. 'Who are you kidding? You could cut the atmosphere with a knife. I thought I'd walked into a force field.'

'Nonsense.' Adrien found her way to the cupboard and took down two beakers and a jar of coffee, moving busily, even fussily, to cover her complete disorientation and her seriously flurried breathing. 'We were simply talking business.'

'That's the kind of business I like.' Zelda gave her a cat-like grin. 'So that's the new model Chay Haddon. Actually, he hasn't changed much. Still blond, still sexy, but definitely more outgoing.' She paused, giving Adrien a speculative glance. 'And you're looking good yourself. Isn't that your new outfit?'

Adrien bit her already sore lip, and winced as she spooned coffee into the beakers and brought the kettle back to the boil. 'We've been out to dinner. I felt I'd better make an effort—that's all.'

'Well—did it work?' Zelda asked with painful intensity.

Adrien stirred the coffee, and tried to get her mind in gear. 'I suppose it did,' she said quietly. 'At any rate he— he's going to pay for the work on the Grange—settle all the bills—and let me finish the project. So, we don't have to worry.'

'Oh, God.' Zelda closed her eyes. 'There is a Santa Claus.' She took a breath, then gave Adrien another penetrating look. 'So, what's the snag?'

'Why should there be one?' Adrien handed over a beaker and took a scalding mouthful of her own brew.

'Because I don't believe in Santa Claus,' Zelda said grimly. 'So, what's the worm in the apple—the fly in the ointment?'

Adrien hesitated. She hadn't time to invent a story, so a half-truth would have to do.

She shrugged, trying to look nonchalant. 'He wants me to move back into the Grange while I'm sorting it out.'

Zelda frowned. 'Why?'

'It's nothing new.' Adrien took another gulp of coffee, hoping that would explain the sudden rush of colour into her face. 'After all, I have been staying there for the past couple of weeks.'

'Yes,' said Zelda. 'But that was when you thought you and Piers were going to be married and the Grange semibelonged to you. That's not the case any more. So, what gives?'

'There's still quite a bit of work to be done,' Adrien parried. 'And he has his own ideas as well. So he wants me on the spot to make sure everything's done properly.'

'Can't he do that for himself?'

'He's away a lot.' Adrien bit her lip. 'Anyway, by paying off the contractors he's got me off the hook, so if he wants a favour I can't really argue about it. I—I owe him.'

'Gratitude is one thing,' said Zelda. 'Although I hope what I interrupted tonight wasn't you simply being grateful,' she added drily. 'But the guy can't expect to own you, body and soul. Remember that.'

Adrien forced a smile. 'Now you're being silly,' she said, surreptitiously crossing her fingers in the folds of her skirt.

But he does own me, she thought, her mind shuddering away from the events of the past half-hour. He does—and there's not a thing I can do about it...

She still could barely believe her reaction to his advances. She had nothing but dislike and contempt for him, and yet she'd stood there and let him do what he wanted without a word of protest, and, but for Zelda's arrival, she would probably be having sex with him at this moment.

I'm as bad as he is, she thought, wincing with distaste.

Zelda spoke, her voice gentle. 'Adie—if you don't want to accept Chay Haddon's offer, say so now. We'll manage somehow. It's not too late.'

Oh, but it is, Adrien thought. It was too late from the moment I saw him standing there, looking up at the house.

'Everything's fine.' She lifted her chin. 'Living at the Grange won't be particularly convenient, but it's only a temporary measure. Soon—very soon—life will be back to normal again.'

And she wished with a kind of dread that she could believe her own reassuring words.

*   *   *

Just a few more hours, Adrien thought, turning the Jeep into the Grange's drive. When the day ended, her life would have changed for ever.

It had been a strange week. The days short, as she'd struggled to finish the Grange. The nights all too long, as sleep had proved elusive.

Do what she would, she had not been able to forget her last encounter with Chay—or forgive herself for it either.

And something told her that she was going to pay dearly for those long moments of self-betrayal in Chay's arms.

She should have insisted that they adhere to the original terms of the bargain—made him leave. Oh, she could see it all now. Why hadn't she been as wise at the time— instead of melting like some sex-starved idiot? she berated herself savagely.

Yet wasn't that exactly what she was?

I'm a throwback, she thought. A total, pathetic anachronism. I don't belong in the twenty-first century.

Looking back, she could see that Piers's determination to postpone the physical consummation of their relationship until they were married hadn't been the act of a chivalrous romantic at all.

He had to sweet-talk me to get me to restore the Grange for him, she thought bleakly. But that was as far as it was ever going to go. The rest of it was my imagination.

She'd lain in the darkness, night after night, trying to remember how Piers's arms had felt—his kisses. And to recall her own responses.

She'd been in love with him, she thought wonderingly, yet, to her shame, not one of his embraces had ever stirred her as Chay's lightest touch had done.

She shivered. How had Chay been able to exert such power over her, and with such consummate ease, too? It seemed too glib to tell herself that he was just a very experienced man toying with the senses of a relatively innocent young woman. But what other explanation was there?

It was almost as if she'd been bewitched.

But next time he wouldn't find her mental and emotional defences so fragile, she promised herself grimly.

She'd found it easier to cope in the daytime. There'd even been times when work on the house had taken her over again. When she'd been able to lose herself in the pleasure of restoration, watching the Grange coming to life again. When she could look around her and allow herself to bask in the satisfaction of a job well done.

All the contractors had returned to work, presumably on Chay Haddon's guarantee, and although she'd been aware of curious glances from some, and an air of constraint from others, no one had referred to the returned cheques, or even to the new ownership. At least not in her hearing.

Sometimes she'd even been able to relegate the price she had to pay for Piers's defection to the back of her mind. Until something would occur to remind her of the new regime, and how intimately she'd soon be involved with it.

The arrival of the phone company to install extra lines and points had been the first thing, and that had been followed by a van-load of high-tech office equipment.

And today she'd been told to expect the arrival of another consignment of furniture.

The first load had arrived the previous day. She'd watched the men carry in chairs and sofas, with luxurious feather cushioning and brocaded covers in sapphire, ivory and jade. They looked good in the formal surroundings of the long drawing room, but she'd been in no mood to admire Chay's taste.

The beds, too, were all brand-new, and ostentatiously large, Adrien had noted, tight-lipped, as she'd directed which rooms they were to be placed in.

She'd chosen a relatively modest queen-size bed for her own quarters, a bedroom with its own tiny shower room and an adjoining sitting room, at the opposite end of the house to Chay's suite.

And today she would complete the furnishing of her little suite. She'd brought an easy chair from the cottage yesterday, but she still needed a chest of drawers and a night table. However, a number of small items of furniture that Piers had deemed not good enough to be auctioned had been relegated to the cellar, so she might find something down there.

Inside the house, the contractors were clearing up and preparing to leave. She'd been astonished at the amount of work they'd got through lately, until she'd heard one of them say that Chay Haddon had promised them all a bonus if they finished on time.

How nice, she thought, to have that kind of money, and to be able to wield that kind of power.

She went into the kitchen and put the kettle on, then took the cellar key from the hook and went off to investigate.

The cellar had once been Angus Stretton's pride and joy, but now it looked more like an explosion in a junk yard, she thought without pleasure, as she switched on the single lightbulb. His collection of wine had been the first thing Piers had sent off for auction.

That should have warned me that he could be short of cash, she thought with an inward sigh. But I believed him when he said he didn't want to live in the past.

But then—what hadn't she believed?

Moving carefully, because the entire place was thick with dust and the spiders had been having a field-day, she began to sort through the hotch-potch of chairs, stools and occasional tables. One of the first things she found was the little davenport that had once stood in the morning room, with one of its delicate pillars snapped off.

That could easily be repaired, she thought, touching it

with a protective finger. Maybe she should make an inventory of everything that was down here.

Underneath a box of odd cups and saucers she came upon a small circular mahogany table, its veneer chipped and scratched but otherwise intact, and a matching chair needing a replacement seat cover. Nearby she unearthed a three-drawer chest, also in mahogany, the bottom draw lacking a handle.

Chay would hardly begrudge her any of those, she thought.

She manhandled the small table up the cellar steps, and was just catching her breath when a voice said, 'Miss Lander?'

She was confronted by a small, rather plump woman in a neat navy suit, with smartly cut grey hair and bright dark eyes.

She said briskly, 'I'm Jean Whitley. I believe you're expecting me.'

Adrien, very conscious of her elderly tee shirt and paint-stained dungarees, gave a constrained smile. 'Yes, of course. Er—welcome to Wildhurst Grange.'

'It's certainly a lovely house.' Mrs Whitley gave her surroundings an appraising look. 'I can see why Mr Haddon feels so strong about it.' She nodded, then picked up the leather suitcase beside her. 'If you'd be good enough to show me my quarters, I'll get settled in. The rest of my things are in the car.'

She looked at her watch. 'Lunch will be ready in an hour and a half, madam. Only soup and sandwiches, I'm afraid, but I'll be back in my stride by this evening.'

She looked at the table. 'And where is that to go?'

'In my room. There are a couple of other things as well,' Adrien said. 'I'm going to ask one of the workmen to bring them up for me.'

'No doubt they'll need cleaning.' Mrs Whitley clicked

her tongue. 'What a shame to let nice things go to rack and ruin. But all that can stop here and now.' She nodded again, rather fiercely. 'Now, where am I to sleep?'

Adrien took her up to the small self-contained flat on the second floor which the Grange housekeepers usually occupied.

I wonder if she knows that Chay used to live there? she wondered as she returned downstairs, feeling as if she'd been caught in a small whirlwind.

The soup was a home-made vegetable broth, and the sandwiches were smoked salmon.

'That was delicious,' Adrien said with complete sincerity when Mrs Whitley arrived to collect her tray.

The housekeeper snorted. 'Nothing but a snack,' she declared, and ran a martial eye over Adrien's slender figure. 'You need feeding up, Miss Lander,' she added, and withdrew.

Did she? Adrien wondered, glimpsing her reflection in the drawing room window. Her week of snatched meals and sleepless nights had emphasised her cheekbones and made her eyes look shadowed and wary. Perhaps Chay would take one look and decide she was past her sell-by date, she thought, her lips twisting wryly.

Mrs Whitley's head reappeared round the door. 'The furniture van's just coming up the drive, madam. Mr Haddon said you'd give the men their orders, as you know where everything goes.'

'I know?' Adrien repeated in bewilderment, following her into the hall. 'I don't understand.'

But comprehension soon came as the first pieces of furniture were carefully unloaded and carried into the house.

She said numbly, 'But those are Mr Stretton's things. That cabinet—and the table and chairs. And there's his big desk from the library.' She shook her head. 'But that's impossible.'

'Not if you know where to look, madam. And Mr Haddon was keen to have the house just as it was in the old days.'

Adrien felt her throat close in shock. My God, she thought, but he's been thorough. He's even got the Persian carpets—and most of the oil paintings too, by the look of it. And the silver...

She opened the nearest crate and found herself looking down at Angus Stretton's chessboard, its ivory and ebony squares gleaming. And next to it was the familiar box of matching chessmen. How many times, she wondered, had she seen Mr Stretton and her father sitting opposite each other in the study, intent on their next moves? And this was the board she'd learned on too.

It's not just the house—or me, she thought, feeling cold. He wants the whole of Piers's inheritance. He hasn't missed a thing. Not the slightest detail.

All these years he must have been waiting. And this is his revenge—on both of us.

She lifted her head, staring into space. Ruthless, she thought. He's totally ruthless. And soon—very soon now—he'll be here. For me.

CHAPTER SIX

'You really don't have to do this,' Zelda said.

Adrien fastened the lid of her suitcase. It had been mid-afternoon before the furniture was finally in place at the Grange, leaving her free to come back to the cottage for her clothes. A task she'd left to the last minute. Like a condemned person hoping for reprieve, she thought ruefully.

She said lightly, 'Oh, but I do. It's a job, just like any other.' She paused. 'My goodness, you didn't make all this fuss when I moved into the Grange last time.'

'That was different,' Zelda said grimly. 'I know it, and you won't admit it.'

'Well, don't look so glum,' Adrien said bracingly, as she hefted her case off the bed. 'I'll be back before you know it. This is our workbase, after all. Besides, I have to see Smudge's puppy.'

'Adie,' Zelda said. 'Tell me you're not doing this so that my son can have a dog.'

'It's work,' Adrien said determinedly. 'Just another assignment. Purely temporary. So don't worry about a thing.'

When Zelda had made her reluctant departure, Adrien carried her case down to the Jeep. She hadn't packed very much, partly because her wardrobe was limited, and far too utilitarian for a tycoon's mistress, she decided with irony, even if she was only on loan. No slinky evening dresses, designer casuals or see-through lingerie anywhere. But perhaps Chay intended to buy her those kind of things, she thought with a grimace.

That could be just one of the many hurdles confronting

her. She still wasn't sure what conclusions Mrs Whitley was drawing about her place in the household, but it hadn't taken long for her to discover that Chay could do no wrong in his housekeeper's eyes, and that she probably wouldn't have turned a hair if Adrien had been lead concubine in his harem.

But she seemed prepared to go along with the fiction that Adrien was just another employee, and had, in a brief time, transformed the rooms Adrien had chosen for herself.

When she got back to the Grange Adrien found the bed made up, two charming watercolours on the sitting room walls, and the reject furniture polished to within an inch of its life. There was a cushion in the easy chair, and a bowl of late roses on the table. Mrs Whitley had even found time to fix new handles to the chest of drawers.

Adrien said, 'It all looks wonderful.'

Mrs Whitley beamed. 'Mr Haddon said I was to make sure you were comfortable and had everything you needed.' She glanced at her watch. 'Now I must make a start on dinner.'

It didn't take long to unpack, and then Adrien found herself at a loose end. It was disturbing to walk round the house and find it almost the same as it had been in Angus Stretton's day. For a small child it had been like a treasure house—an enchanted castle with Mr Stretton as the kindly wizard, talking to her about the pictures on the walls, opening the cabinets of curios so that she could hold them while he told her their history. And always Chay had been there, a quiet, watchful presence on the edge of her vision.

Mr Stretton was so good to him, Adrien thought wretchedly. It must have broken his heart to find that he was a thief.

Thank God he can never know that Chay was just biding his time, she told herself with bitterness. That he's stepped in and stolen everything.

The afternoon seemed endless, moving slowly but inevitably to the moment when Chay would return.

She tried to keep herself occupied, using the computer in the office to draw up a new design for the kitchen garden, but got to a point where the walls of the room seemed to be closing in on her. She was glancing at her watch every few seconds, every nerve on edge and screaming, so that at last she said, 'To hell with it,' and went out for a walk instead.

She went up through the trees, steadfastly ignoring the place where the treehouse used to be. She had to dismiss that part of her childhood—relegate it to some distant corner of her mind—even though the sense of betrayal—of desertion—would always haunt her.

What Piers had done to her was infinitely worse, yet some strange instinct told her that his defection would not linger nearly as long in her mind. And that made no sense at all.

The sun was still warm on her back, but there was a crispness in the air which signalled autumn. It was her favourite time of year, and one of the busiest too, as people decided to have rooms redone for Christmas. But now Chay Haddon had the right to the lion's share of her time.

But I can't allow the business to suffer, she told herself. I'll need something to go back to when—all this is over.

She bit her lip and increased her stride. It was the present she needed to worry about, she reminded herself grimly. The future—well, that would have to look after itself.

It was over an hour later when she got back to the house, and Mrs Whitley met her with an air of faint reproach.

'Mr Haddon called,' she said. 'He's been slightly delayed, so I've put dinner back to eight-thirty.' She paused. 'Would you like me to run you a bath, madam? And bring you a glass of sherry, perhaps?'

My God, thought Adrien. She thinks I'm going to do the

whole bit. Soak in a hot tub, rub in body lotion, varnish my toenails, and put on something glamorous and revealing. Prepare myself for the master's return.

Well, no chance. That's not for me. In my case, what you see is what you get.

She smiled at Mrs Whitley. 'Thanks, but I'm just going to have a quick shower. And I'll have a glass of white wine—Chardonnay, for preference—when I come down.'

'Just as you wish, madam, of course. But I thought...'

'I'm sure you did,' said Adrien, and ran lightly up the stairs.

So she wasn't deceived at all, she thought, wondering just how many others Mrs Whitley had pampered in this particular way...

Wrinkling her nose, she went into her room and banged the door with unnecessary force.

She showered and washed her hair, then pulled on a pair of white jeans and a black silky sweater with long sleeves and a round neck before piling her still-damp hair into a loose topknot. She put on moisturiser, added a coating of mascara to her lashes, and a pale coral lustre to her lips.

Tidy, she decided, giving herself a critical look. And that was all the effort she was prepared to make.

Reluctantly, she went downstairs, into the drawing room. The lamps had been lit and there was a fire burning in the hearth, dispelling the faint chill of the evening. The whole room seemed to be glowing a welcome, Adrien thought cynically, taking a seat on one of the jewel-colour sofas. And the only discordant note was herself.

Now that the moment of truth had finally come, she could feel tension coiling inside her. She could rationalise what she was doing until the crack of doom, but the fact remained that tonight she had a debt to pay. And the transaction would take place in Chay's bed. In Chay's arms.

And she wasn't sure she could cope. If she could bear the reality of it.

As if, she thought bitterly, she had a choice.

She was grateful for the wine that she'd found cooling on a side table. It was cool and fragrant against her dry throat, but she wasn't going to drink too much of it. That had been the cause of her problems last time, she told herself with conviction, and she couldn't risk another loss of control like that.

While she was getting ready, she'd reached a serious decision. Chay would have the access to her body that he'd paid for, but nothing more. Because her heart and soul belonged to herself alone. That was the only way she could survive. By closing off her mind, by divorcing herself from everything but the physical act.

Endurance, she thought, staring at the restless flames curling round the logs in the dog crate. That was the word to focus on. To cling to.

Mrs Whitley came bustling in, smiling. 'Mr Haddon has returned, madam. He's gone up to change. Perhaps you'd like to take his drink up to him. He has whisky with a little spring water,' she added confidentially.

She paused expectantly, and Adrien, whose lips had started to frame a blistering retort, found herself subsiding, the furious words bitten back.

This, she thought, was how it began. What she had to expect. And there was no point in protesting. It was, after all, only what she'd agreed to.

She swallowed hard. 'Very well,' she said tonelessly, and took the heavy cut-glass tumbler which Mrs Whitley was holding out to her.

'And do you still wish me to serve dinner at half past eight, madam?' The question was delicately put but the implication was clear, and Adrien felt her face burn.

She said coolly, 'Yes, that will be fine, thanks,' and started for the door.

Her legs were like lead as she mounted the stairs and walked along the passage to the master suite at the end.

She would knock, she thought, leave the whisky on his night table, then make herself scarce. And Mrs Whitley could read what she wanted into that.

She tapped gently at the door, and opened it a fraction. The bedroom appeared to be empty, and she could hear the sound of running water coming from the bathroom.

The coast was clear, she thought, treading quietly across the room. She was just about to place the whisky beside the bed when Chay spoke from behind her. 'Good evening.'

Adrien jumped violently, spilling a few drops of spirits on the carpet, then turned warily to face him.

He was standing in the bathroom doorway, towelling his shoulders and upper arms. And, apart from another towel draped casually round his hips, he was naked.

Against the white towel, his skin looked very brown. It was the kind of all-over tan he certainly wouldn't have acquired in Brussels, she thought, biting her lip.

She said huskily, 'You—you startled me.'

'I seem to make a habit of it,' he returned drily, running his fingers through his water-darkened hair. 'And you're quite a surprise yourself. Is that drink for me? How sweet and thoughtful of you.'

'It isn't— I mean, I didn't...' Adrien stumbled to a halt, resentfully aware of the amusement lurking in his grey eyes. 'Mrs Whitley asked me to bring it.'

'Ah,' he said softly. 'But Jean always did have a romantic streak.' There was a note of laughter in his voice, and something else, less easily definable.

He tossed the towel he was using for his hair back into the bathroom and took a step forward. Adrien froze.

He paused, his mouth twisting wryly. He said, 'Adrien,

I'm going to comb my hair. That's all. And it may comfort you to know that I never ravish women on an empty stomach. You're safe until after dinner.'

She said unevenly, 'You bastard—how dare you laugh at me?'

'I was trying to be reassuring—as the sight of me seems to have turned you to stone.' He walked to his dressing table and picked up a comb. 'You'll have to get used to it, Adrien.'

'Used to what?'

'Having me around—with or without my clothes.' He was watching her in the mirror. 'Or have you changed your mind about our bargain?'

She lifted her chin. 'I'm here, aren't I?'

'Ah, yes,' he said. 'But that's not the same thing at all. You've had nearly a week to think again.'

She said shortly, 'I can't afford second thoughts, and you know it.'

'Well, you're honest.' He put the comb down and turned. 'So, bring my drink over here, please—and say hello to me properly.'

Reluctantly, she complied, heart sinking, stomach churning, and mouth as dry as a desert. Chay took the tumbler from her hand and put it down, then let his fingers curl gently round the nape of her neck, drawing her forward.

His skin smelt cool and damp, the fragrance of soap commingling with the sharper essence of some cologne.

He said softly, 'You can fake your orgasm later, darling. For now, just pretend to be glad to see me.' And his mouth took hers.

She stood in the circle of his arms, steeling herself against the gently insidious movement of his lips on hers, her body taut as a bowstring under the skilful glide of his hands.

He lifted his head and stared down at her, the grey eyes

glittering. He said, 'I told you I'd expect my money's worth, Adrien. And so far you haven't earned a penny. So—relax.'

He put up a hand and took the clips from her hair, letting it fall to her shoulders, his fingers teasing the damp, silky strands. Then he took her hands, lifting them to his shoulders.

He said softly, 'Touch me.'

Swallowing, Adrien obeyed, her fingers spreading over the smooth skin, feeling the hard muscularity that lay beneath. A tacit reminder of how helpless she really was. Of how easily he could subdue her if she tried to fight...

Chay kissed her again more deeply, parting her unwilling lips with his and exploring the softness of her mouth with his tongue.

His hands slid down to her hips, pulling her against him, letting her experience the strength and heated power of his arousal.

The thin layers of cloth which separated them were no barrier—no barrier at all, she thought, as her breathing quickened and her lashes swept down to veil her eyes.

When he lifted his head, he was smiling faintly. 'You see,' he said. 'This is not going to be as impossible as you think.'

Adrien stared up at him. She felt strangely dizzy, as if she'd taken some powerful drug.

She said, her voice shaking, 'I hate you.'

He nodded, unperturbed. 'I can live with that. At least you're not claiming to have fallen madly in love with me. Because that could mean serious trouble.

'And leave your hair loose,' he added sharply, as Adrien dived to retrieve her clips from the floor. The look he sent her was sardonic. 'It will give me something to fantasise about while I'm dressing.'

She glared at him. 'Am I free to go now?'

'The choice, as always, is yours, my sweet.' He picked up the tumbler of whisky and lifted it in a mocking toast. 'But if you stay, dinner could be delayed indefinitely. My appetite seems to have changed.' He swallowed some whisky and put the glass down again, his eyes quizzical as his hands moved to discard the towel round his hips.

He said softly, his gaze holding hers. 'Well, Adie, what's it to be?'

She gasped in outrage and whirled round, making for the door. And as she fled, to her chagrin, she heard his laughter following her.

She was still ruffled some twenty minutes later, seated tensely on the edge of one of the sofas, the stem of her wine glass gripped so tightly it was in danger of snapping.

How could he do this? she asked herself despairingly. How was it possible that, just for a fleeting moment— barely more than a second, indeed—she'd been tempted? That she'd actually wondered, to her shame, what it would be like to have that potent male force sheathed inside her…?

And he—Chay Haddon—had evoked this unlooked for sexual curiosity in her. Had deliberately initiated this need to know—and be known.

'Damn him,' she said raggedly under her breath. 'Oh, damn him to hell.'

'I hope I haven't kept you waiting.' Right on cue, he was there, watching her from the doorway.

Adrien stared back, lifting her chin insolently. 'Please don't apologise,' she said. 'It must have been quite a fantasy.'

'The best.' Chay strolled across to the drinks table and replenished his glass. 'Remind me to share it with you some time.' He indicated the bottle of Chardonnay. 'Some more wine?'

She said hurriedly, 'No—thank you.'

He said silkily, 'I'm sure you're wise.'

She raised her eyebrows. 'You want me sober?'

'Not necessarily,' he said. 'But conscious would be a bonus.'

As he walked across the room, Adrien tensed involuntarily, but he made no attempt to join her, choosing instead the sofa on the opposite side of the fireplace.

He moved well, she acknowledged unwillingly, his body lean and graceful. But even as a boy he hadn't been subject to the usual adolescent gaucherie.

Only, they weren't children any longer. And he was a predator with his prey in sight. She had to remember that.

He'd gone for the casual look, too, in blue denim, the shirt open at the neck to reveal the faint shadowing of chest hair that she remembered had felt like springing silk beneath her fingers. The cuffs were turned back negligently over tanned forearms, and his legs in the close-fitting jeans seemed to go on for ever.

She watched him lean back against the cushions, very much at ease, his dark blond hair gleaming like silk in the lamplight. Making himself at home, she thought, igniting anger and resentment inside her and letting it burn slowly, driving out the trembling weakness which the sight of him had induced.

The intruder, she whispered silently. The usurper. Something else she could not afford to forget.

He said softly, 'So you're still here.'

She stared down at her empty glass. 'Did you doubt it?'

'I wasn't totally certain.' A smile played round his mouth. 'That's one of your great charms, Adie. Your ability to surprise me.'

She said curtly, 'I must try to become more predictable.'

'You just did,' he murmured, and she subsided, biting her lip.

There was a silence as he sipped his Scotch and took a long, appraising look round the room. He said, 'The house looks good. Thank you.'

Adrien shrugged. 'It wasn't difficult to achieve.' She paused. 'I have a good memory.'

'If a selective one,' he murmured.

'You seem to have instant recall, too,' she went on doggedly, deliberately ignoring his interjection. 'You've hardly missed a thing. How on earth did you do it?' She gave a small, harsh laugh. 'You must have been stalking Piers for weeks.'

'I didn't have to.' He lifted his glass, studying the amber of the whisky with a kind of detached appreciation. 'I knew what he would do, and the probable markets he would use. After that, it was simple.'

'Easy pickings,' she said stonily. 'Like everything else you've taken from him. He really didn't stand a chance.'

He drank some whisky. 'I didn't exactly hold him at gunpoint.' His tone was unexpectedly mild. 'He chose to sell. And I'm a little surprised to find that you're still defending him.'

'I'm not,' Adrien denied. 'I just don't understand why you should have gone trawling through the salerooms for Angus's furniture. What were you trying to prove?'

'Not a thing. I simply wanted his things back where they belong. I thought if he knew, he'd be pleased.' He paused. 'I thought you'd be glad, too.'

'Pleased that you rescued them? When you abused the roof he put over your head?' Her voice bit. 'When he barred you from his house for thieving?' She shook her head. 'I think it would make him sick to his stomach to know that you're here—pretending to be the master.'

'And is that how you feel, too?'

Across the space that divided them their eyes met and clashed. His gaze was like grey ice, but there was something darker, deeper, that quickened her breath, shivering along her nerve-endings, and Adrien was the first to look away.

She said hoarsely, 'What else?'

'Then that's unfortunate,' he said softly. 'Because I am the master here—be in no doubt of that, Adrien.' He paused, allowing his words to sink in, watching her pupils dilate in confusion as she absorbed them.

'Now,' he continued coldly, 'I've had one hell of a day, and a bastard of a journey, so I really don't need this.'

He flung the remains of the whisky down his throat and got to his feet. 'Shall we go to dinner—or are you planning a hunger strike?'

For a crazy moment she was tempted to do just that. To run. To take refuge in her room and lock the door.

But something told her that he would follow, and that might precipitate a disaster which could haunt her for the rest of her life.

Not in anger, she thought, swallowing convulsively. I— I couldn't bear to be taken in anger.

She stood up, lifting her chin, because she didn't want him to sense the naked panic twisting inside her, and went with him, in silence, to the dining room.

Play the Lucky Hearts Game

and get...

2 FREE BOOKS
and a FREE MYSTERY GIFT...
YOURS to KEEP!

yes! I have scratched off the silver card. Please send me my *2 FREE BOOKS* and *FREE mystery GIFT*. I understand that I am under no obligation to purchase any books as explained on the back of this card.

Scratch Here!

then look below to see what your cards get you... 2 Free Books & a Free Mystery Gift!

306 HDL DU6W   **106 HDL DU7E**

FIRST NAME

LAST NAME

ADDRESS

APT.#

CITY

STATE/PROV.

ZIP/POSTAL CODE

(H-P-08/03)

Twenty-one gets you
2 FREE BOOKS
and a *FREE MYSTERY GIFT!*

Twenty gets you
2 FREE BOOKS!

Nineteen gets you
1 FREE BOOK!

TRY AGAIN!

◀ DETACH AND MAIL CARD TODAY! ▶

The Harlequin Reader Service® — Here's how it works:

Accepting your 2 free books and mystery gift places you under no obligation to buy anything. You may keep the books and gift and return the shipping statement marked "cancel." If you do not cancel, about a month later we'll send you 6 additional books and bill you just $3.57 each in the U.S., or $4.24 each in Canada, plus 25¢ shipping & handling per book and applicable taxes if any.* That's the complete price and — compared to cover prices of $4.25 each in the U.S. and $4.99 each in Canada — it's quite a bargain! You may cancel at any time, but if you choose to continue, every month we'll send you 6 more books, which you may either purchase at the discount price or return to us and cancel your subscription.

*Terms and prices subject to change without notice. Sales tax applicable in N.Y. Canadian residents will be charged applicable provincial taxes and GST. Credit or debit balances in a customer's account(s) may be offset by any other outstanding balance owed by or to the customer.

CHAPTER SEVEN

THE CENTRAL leaves had been removed from the big dining table, and candles had been lit to provide a more intimate atmosphere. Mrs Whitley was a determined woman, Adrien thought without amusement. Or perhaps she had her orders...

Chay saw Adrien to her chair, then seated himself opposite.

'Not quite two sword lengths apart,' he observed drily. 'But you should be safe enough.'

Adrien concentrated on shaking out her table napkin. 'Safe,' she thought, was not a word she could ever apply to her present situation.

It's a business transaction, she reminded herself forcibly, adding the mantra she'd been whispering to herself all week. Nothing lasts for ever...

Mrs Whitley had provided a marvellous meal—a home-made country pâté, followed by duck with a dark cherry sauce, and crème brûlée to finish with.

To her surprise, Adrien found she was enjoying the food, and the claret that accompanied it. Ironic, she thought, that her appetite should have chosen this of all days to return.

It wasn't a silent meal, although Chay initiated most of the conversation, talking lightly about his trip to Brussels, and the problems with European bureaucracy. At any other time she'd have been intrigued and animated, leaning forward to ask questions, or expand on a point he'd made.

We could always talk to each other once, she thought with a sudden pang. But that was while I was a child, and

didn't know any better. When I trusted him. Before everything changed...

She found herself wondering how she would feel if they
had just met for the first time. If she was here with him
now simply because she wanted to be, without the past like
a shadow at her shoulder.

But she couldn't let herself think like that. It was stupid—and could be dangerous, she reflected with a slight
shiver.

'Are you cold?' He didn't miss a thing.

'No—I'm fine.' It was the usual all-purpose lie, and it
was a relief when Mrs Whitley appeared to clear the table
before Chay could probe any further.

The housekeeper returned briefly, to bring in coffee and
armagnac, and then withdrew, wishing them goodnight.

'She's very discreet,' Adrien said, after a pause. 'But I
suppose she'd had a lot of practice.'

Chay sighed. 'What do you want me to say?' he asked
wearily. 'That I've been celibate all these years? It wouldn't
be true.'

'And, naturally, you're the soul of honesty,' she said
bitterly.

'But there hasn't been a constant procession of women
through my life either,' he went on, as if she hadn't spoken.
'A major part of my time has been taken up by work—
getting the company established abroad as well as here.'

'Oh, don't let's forget for a minute what a dazzling success you are.' Her voice was heavy with sarcasm. 'Yet you
never seemed particularly ambitious in the old days.'

He shrugged. 'Perhaps I was still deciding what I really
wanted.'

'And it just turned out to be Piers's inheritance.'

His smile was cold. 'Piers was only ever interested in
disposable assets. Haven't you grasped that yet?'

'He was in trouble, and you dangled a small fortune in front of him. What was he supposed to do?'

'In his place, I wouldn't have sold.' He paused, then added more gently, 'And nor would you, Adrien.'

She found his use of her name disturbing. The way his voice seemed to linger over the syllables sent an odd, unwelcome frisson down her spine.

She looked down at her cup, aware that his eyes were on her, feeling her heart begin to bang unevenly against her ribcage.

He said, 'Shall we take our coffee into the drawing room?'

She touched the tip of her tongue to her dry lips. 'It's fine here—isn't it?'

'You mean with a yard or two of solid oak between us?' He was openly amused. 'Believe me, my sweet, the barricade you're trying to build in that stubborn mind of yours is far more effective.'

She flushed. 'I don't know what you're talking about.'

'Don't lie, Adrien.' Chay leaned forward. There were little silver sparks dancing in his eyes, she noted confusedly, or was it just some trick of the light? 'Right this moment, there's a battle going on between your heart and your body. That's why you're spitting venom at me with every other breath.'

She said very clearly, 'Of course it couldn't be that I just don't find you attractive?'

'In that case,' he said, his voice almost meditative, 'why don't you wear a bra when I'm around?'

She gasped, and her colour deepened fierily. 'How—how dare you? I do as I like.'

'But not all the time.' He slanted a grin at her. 'You were wearing one that first day, but not later—when we went out to dinner. I—er—noticed particularly,' he added, his grin deepening reminiscently. 'And you're not wearing one tonight either. Interesting, don't you think?'

'Only if your mind's in the gutter,' she hit back.

'Why, Adie,' he said gently. 'What a little hypocrite you are.' He picked up his coffee and got to his feet. 'Now, I'm going to sit in my new drawing room and listen to some music. I suggest you go to bed.' He paused. 'In your own room.'

Her lips parted in sheer astonishment as she stared up at him. 'But I thought... I don't understand.'

Chay shrugged. 'What's to understand?' he countered. 'This is your own private war that you're fighting, darling, and although I'm naturally interested in the outcome, I haven't the patience tonight to become personally involved. For which you should be grateful,' he added with grim significance. 'As I said, I've had a bastard of a day, and I'm not turning my bed into a battlefield. So, when the fight's over let me know which won—your mind or your body. Because it matters quite a lot.'

He paused on his way to the door and swung round, his eyes raking her mercilessly. 'And forgive me for not kissing you goodnight, my sweet. I think it's best to keep my distance, or I might forget myself and show you that the top of that table isn't quite the defence against passion that you seem to think. Catch my drift?'

He nodded to her with a kind of remote courtesy, and left, closing the door behind him quietly but very definitely.

Leaving her sitting there. Staring after him. Trying to make sense of what had just happened.

There were a number of emotions struggling for dominance inside her, but disbelief was ahead on points.

All evening he'd been making love to her with his eyes, his voice, his smile. She'd assumed he'd be offering a more physical expression before long, and had been gearing herself up for passive resistance. And now—nothing.

So, what sort of game was he playing?

She shouldn't ask questions, she thought, as she pinched out the candles and walked slowly to the door in her turn. She should just be thankful. But gratitude didn't seem to feature too strongly in her inner turmoil.

She could hear music from the drawing room as she crossed the hall. Rachmaninov, she recognised, passionate and plangent. Not the cool jazz she'd expected.

But let's face it, Adie, she told herself. You don't know what to expect any more. And she went upstairs to her room. Alone.

That night she dreamed about the treehouse again. The same dream as always, where she knelt on rough boards, peering, terrified, over the edge, searching for a way down. But the ground, hundreds of feet below, was shrouded in clouds and mist, and she knew she was seeking a safety—a reassurance—that no longer existed. Knew, too, that it wasn't simply the isolation or distance from the ground that was scaring her...

She could hear herself crying, but barely recognised her own voice. There were other voices too, raised in anger, but she couldn't catch the words as a rising wind took the little house and shook it, sending it tumbling down into crumpled matchwood. And her with it.

Adrien awoke with a start, to find tears on her face. She sat up shakily and looked at her alarm clock, and saw it had just gone one a.m.

She drank some water from the carafe on her night table, then got out of bed, wandering across to the window seat.

Tucking her feet under her, she leaned her forehead against the cool pane and stared sightlessly into the darkness.

It was time, she thought, to lay some ghosts to rest. To force herself to remember exactly what had happened all those years ago and then wipe it from her mind. If she could.

Young as she'd been, she'd sensed instantly the hostility between Chay and Piers from the first day the glamorous newcomer had spent at the Grange, and had been distressed by it. Chay had been her friend, but Piers was exciting, almost alien, with his expensive clothes and easy charm.

'So this is the demon chess-player,' he greeted her at their first meeting. 'My uncle's told me all about you. I shall have to watch my step.'

And when they played, and she beat him, he praised her extravagantly, making her glow. Each time she went to the Grange after that he sought her out, behaving as if she was the one person he wanted to see.

She tried her best to bring the two boys together. She wanted them to like each other so that she wouldn't feel disloyal when Piers monopolised her company, as he undoubtedly did. But Chay stayed aloof.

And it wasn't Piers's fault. He was clearly interested in Chay, continually asking questions about him. And, eventually, Adrien succumbed to his pressure and showed him the treehouse.

She knew at once it was a mistake. She stood, awkward and upset, while Piers prowled round, examining everything with contemptuous eyes, rifling through the precious biscuit tin, tossing the neat pile of sketches on to the plank floor.

'Field glasses.' He snatched them up. 'Good ones too. Where did he pinch these from?'

'Mr Stretton gave them to him.' Adrien looked apprehensively at the entrance. 'Let's go down again, please. Chay will be angry if he finds us here. It's his special place.'

'Chay has no right to any place at all.' There was a note in his voice that scared her. 'He's nothing—just the housekeeper's son.' He looked down at the field glasses. 'As for these...' His arm went back, and he hurled them into the nearby trees. She heard a crash and a tinkle as they landed.

She said with a little wail, 'You've broken them,' and began to scramble down. But when she reached the ground Chay was waiting, his face like stone and his eyes bitter with anger and condemnation as he looked at Adrien.

She tried to say something, but he cut her short. 'Go back to the house, Adie. Go now.'

Tears streaming down her face, she ran. Behind her, she could hear angry voices, then the violent sound of a scuffle. As she came out of the trees she saw her father standing with Angus Stretton by the gateway to the kitchen garden, clearly looking for her. She reached them breathlessly.

'Chay and Piers are fighting,' she gasped through her tears. 'Oh, make them stop—please.'

Mr Stretton said grimly, 'I'll deal with it,' and broke into a run.

'We'd better go home,' her father said, trying to hustle her gently away, but she resisted.

'No, Daddy, please. I want to see Chay. I want to see he's not hurt.'

She watched them come down from the trees, with Angus Stretton bringing up the rear.

Piers, looking thunderous, had a split lip and a torn shirt, while Chay, staring in front of him, his face set, had the beginnings of a black eye.

Adrien twisted free of her father's restraining hand and ran up to him. 'Chay.' Her voice was urgent. 'Chay, I'm sorry. I didn't mean it to happen—any of it.'

He didn't look at her, and his voice was barely more than a whisper. 'Go away from me, Adie, and keep away. I'm warning you.'

But she had to see him, she thought as she lay in bed

that night. She had to talk to him properly and explain. Tell him how sorry she was that their secret place was spoiled.

The next morning she told her mother she was going to play with a schoolfriend, who lived at the other end of the village, and set off on her bike, taking the back road to the Grange instead.

She left her bike in a deserted corner of the rear yard and set off to the wood, expecting to find Chay already there, clearing up.

By the time she reached the tree the sky had darkened, and misty rain was falling. Usually he helped her to climb up, but this time there was no answer when she called, so she had to struggle up as best she could, her feet slipping on the damp rungs.

Chay had already been there, she saw with disappointment, because all his things had gone. The little structure looked deserted and forlorn. All that remained was one sketch, torn in half and lying face-down on the floor.

When Adrien picked it up she realised it was a drawing of herself, lying on her tummy with her chin propped in her hands. She hadn't even known he was sketching her, and now he didn't want it any more, she thought desolately.

She was standing staring at it, tears pricking at the backs of her eyes, when she heard a scraping noise from down below. Puzzled, she went to the edge and peeped down cautiously, only to see the ladder lying on the ground and someone walking away. A figure in a grey waterproof hooded coat as familiar to her as her own green anorak.

Bewildered, and frightened, she shouted to him. 'Chay— I can't get down. Come back—oh, please come back.'

But he didn't even look round. Just kept going until he was lost to view among the trees. And although she went on calling until her voice was hoarse, her only answer was silence.

When Piers found her at last, hours later, Chay was with

him, still wearing that betraying grey jacket, and somehow that was the worst thing of all.

She screamed at him, 'You did this! I saw you! I hate you!' And she picked up the stone and threw it at him.

She saw the blood on his cheek, and the grey eyes turn to chips of ice. And realised she had lost her friend for ever.

Adrien came back, shivering, to the present, to find that her arms were wrapped protectively round her body. Each memory, it seemed, still had claws to tear her apart.

How could he do that? she asked herself stormily. I was a thoughtless child. I didn't deserve that. He didn't care that I was frightened. Didn't think that I could have fallen and hurt myself badly—or even been killed.

She'd been taken home and fussed over, given a hot bath and warm milk, and been tucked into bed. But she hadn't been able to sleep, and she'd got up and gone to her parents' room. The door had been ajar, and she'd heard them talking in low voices.

'The boy's dangerous,' her father had been saying. 'Angus has always been afraid of something like this.'

She hadn't been able to hear her mother's response, only her father's incisive, 'Oh, he'll be sent away, of course. There's no alternative.'

And the next day Chay had been gone from the Grange. She'd told herself she was glad. That she never wanted to see him again.

But he'd come back, of course, bringing different trouble with him.

And now he was here to stay, and more dangerous than ever. Because she was in his power, trapped again, with no means of escape apart from the terms he himself had offered.

Terms she'd accepted, and now had to fulfil. Before it

was too late, and his patience was exhausted. Or his transient desire for her passed...

She slid down from the seat, her face fixed and set. Nothing could change the past, but she needed to make sure her future was secure. Too much depended on the deal she'd made with Chay, and now she had to keep her side of it.

The peignoir she'd bought for her honeymoon was in the wardrobe, swathed in tissue. Without giving herself time to think again, Adrien pulled her cotton nightshirt over her head and dropped it on the floor. The gossamer ivory peignoir spilled into her hands for a long moment.

So fragile, she thought. So transparent. Wearing it, a woman would have no defences. Seeing it, a man would have no doubts.

Swallowing, she put it on, tying the ribbons that fastened it at throat and waist.

The silk whispered round her as she left her room and went silently down the corridor.

He would probably be asleep, she thought, with self-derision. And her grand gesture of capitulation would be totally wasted.

But he was awake, propped up on one elbow and reading. The dark green coverlet had been pushed back, and a sheet just covered the curve of his lean hip. Beneath it he was clearly naked, and it occurred to her that she'd never seen a naked man before. Apart from pictures, she amended dizzily, and no amount of paint or film could ever have prepared her for the warm, living reality.

She thought she hadn't made a sound, but his head lifted instantly, sharply, and he stared at her, marking the place in his book with a finger.

He said softly, 'Insomnia would seem to be catching.'

'Yes.' Her voice was husky. She felt heat rise in her face, flood through her body under the sensuous intensity of his gaze.

'The hot drinks are in the kitchen,' he said after a pause. 'I don't use sleeping pills. So, what can I do for you, Adrien?' It sounded like a civil question. The courteous host enquiring after the well-being of a guest. Only she knew differently...

'Chay.' Her voice broke huskily. 'Don't make this more difficult than it has to be.'

He leaned back against the pillows, watching her from under lowered lids. 'The problem's all in your mind, Adrien. It always has been. Ever since you decided I was your enemy.'

'I was a child,' she said. 'A little girl.'

'Not you, my pet. You were a woman the moment you were born. I watched you grow up—remember?' He touched a hand mockingly to his cheek. 'It scarred me for life.'

'You're not the only one with scars,' she said. 'Those hours I spent in the treehouse still give me nightmares. I— I had one earlier tonight.'

'If you've come here to be comforted,' he said, with a touch of harshness, 'think again.'

She said steadily. 'You know why I'm here.'

His smile mocked faintly. 'You look like a bride on her wedding night. But appearances can be deceptive.'

Her throat tightened. 'That cuts both ways. I don't know who you are any more. Or what you are.'

He shrugged a tanned shoulder. 'I'm a man whose money you need. I thought we'd established that.'

He closed his book and put it on the night table with a certain finality, then took one of the pillows from behind him and tossed it on to the bed at his side. Turned back the edge of the sheet in invitation.

He said softly, 'Well, make your move, darling. I'm all attention.'

She paused helplessly. 'Will you—turn off the lamp—please?'

'No,' he said. 'I want to look at you. You can't walk in here wearing something as revealing as that exquisite piece of nonsense then play the modesty card. So take it off, my lovely one, and walk towards me. Slowly.'

'You don't understand.' She hesitated, her hand on the ribbon at her throat. 'I've never—I mean, I'm not into casual sex.'

'Who said this was going to be casual?' The grey eyes seemed to burn into hers. 'Now come here, or do I have to fetch you?'

She'd never been naked in front of a man before either, she thought as she loosened the ribbons. And she'd been crazy to think she could stay detached—treat this as some routine task.

She wanted it to be dark, so that she didn't have to see the stark hunger in his face. She wanted silence, so she couldn't hear the sudden harsh breath he drew as she let the peignoir fall from her shoulders. She wanted it finished, so that she would never feel so helpless and so—stupid again.

She was aware of every hammering pulse-beat in her body. Could feel the dark race of her own blood as she walked to the bed. There was an iron bar constricting her chest—or was that just because she was holding her breath?

When she reached the bed, she sank down on to it, her hands gripping the edge of the mattress. She bent her head, letting her hair fall forward and shield her flushed face. And waited.

She thought she heard him sigh, then sensed movement and realised that he was kneeling behind her. She tensed, but his fingers were gentle, brushing her hair from her neck, exposing the sensitive nape to the warmth of his lips. She moved restively, surprised—disturbed—at the shiver of reaction that feathered through her, and felt his hands close on her shoulders, stilling her.

His mouth moved slowly downward, covering the taut skin over her shoulderblades, then beginning to trace, softly and sensuously, the long, delicate line of her spine.

Adrien released her pent-up breath in a gasp that was only part shock, her back arching in response to his caress. He pulled her back towards him so that she was leaning against him, the heat of his body penetrating her frozen inner core of panic and shame, dissolving it slowly away.

His arms encircled her, his hands sliding down to enjoy the involuntary thrust of her breasts, the long fingers moulding their softness while the palms moved in aching provocation against her hardening nipples.

Her head fell back on his shoulder, allowing him to kiss her throat, and she felt the hot flicker of his tongue in the whorls of her ear.

She was trembling in earnest now, but not with fear, consumed by a maelstrom of other far more unwelcome emotions. Her throat muscles were quivering under the caress of his mouth. Her breasts were swelling, blossoming with excitement under the subtle play of his fingers, and this wasn't how she'd planned it at all.

She hadn't bargained for her own curiosity, she thought dazedly. For the frustrations of her relationship with Piers. It was those dreams, those longings which had awoken her. It had to be.

Because it couldn't be the hands and lips of the man who was holding her. Who was turning her gently in his embrace, lowering her to the pillow so that she was lying beside him—beneath him—his nakedness grazing hers. Whose mouth was seeking hers, caressing her lips, then coaxing her lips apart to accept the heated silk of his tongue.

His hands clasped hers, raising them above her head so

that he could feast on the satin skin of her underarms, while his leg slid across, covering both of hers, pinning her to the bed, so that she could not have moved even if she'd wanted to.

Making her realise, to her shame, that it was the last thing she wanted.

Then he began to kiss her breasts, adoring their scented roundness, letting his lips tug softly at her nipples, sending shafts of sensation racing like tiny flames through her restless body.

She found she was lifting herself towards him, mutely begging for the sweet agony of his tongue against the rosy engorged peaks.

Chay sighed again, this time with soft satisfaction, his breath fanning her heated skin as he pleasured her.

He'd released her hands, and now she felt the lingering whisper of his fingers on her body, discovering every curve and angle on their slow downward path.

His hands moulded her hipbone, then slid inward to the soft pulsating hollow, where he paused.

She was caught, held tantalisingly on some unimagined brink. She tried to say, No, but all that emerged was a tiny sound like a whimper, while that too was stifled by his kiss.

His hand was at the junction of her thighs, stroking the silky triangle of hair, silently teasing her into allowing him the more intimate access he wanted. And she could feel her body melting, the responding rush of scalding heat that welcomed the first devastating glide of his fingers.

The breath came sobbing from her lungs as his exploration of her deepened, creating a need—a reaction—that she could not control. Her body was opening for him, demanding him, so that when he moved across her—over her—his hands lifting her hips to meet the burning force of his possession, denial was impossible.

It was so right, so totally imperative, that Adrien had no

inkling that her inexperienced flesh might resist this initial
invasion. The sudden unexpected pain jolted her into a
small shocked cry, her eyes dilating as she tried, too late,
to push him away from her.

He said, 'Adrien?' his voice harsh and urgent, then the
bewilderment in his face changed to a kind of horrified
comprehension.

He groaned her name again, but this time it was a plea
for forgiveness as his driven body, establishing its ownership beyond question or control, was impelled towards the
point of no return.

She closed her eyes, pressing a clenched fist against her
mouth as, at last, she felt the frenzied spasms tearing him
apart, and heard him cry out in a kind of agony.

Then it was over, his body sinking against hers in heavy
quietude, the hoarseness of his breathing slowing to normality.

She lay, unmoving, unable to differentiate between the
ache of her wrenched body and the sharper pain of disappointment twisting inside her, and a single tear squeezed
from under her closed lid and burned its way down her
cheek.

She saw him wince, then silently take the corner of the
sheet and wipe the tear away. Then he lifted himself away
from her, putting space between them on the bed.

There was a long pause, then he said very quietly, 'Why
didn't you tell me, Adie?'

'I didn't think you'd know.' She bit her lip. 'And I
thought it wouldn't matter.'

'But you're wrong,' he said. 'Because it makes one hell
of a difference, and in all kinds of ways.'

'I—I don't see how.' She drew a quick, shaky breath.
'This was what we agreed.'

His mouth tightened. 'I could at least have made it—
easier for you.' There was another silence, then he said

slowly, 'I assumed, you see, that you'd slept with Mendoza.'

'He said we'd wait.' Her voice trembled. 'He said he wanted a white wedding—and a wedding night that meant something.'

He nodded, his face like a stone. 'And that's what you should have had, Adie.' He sighed harshly. 'Oh, God, what a bloody mess.'

She turned her head on the pillow and looked at him. He was so careful, she thought, not to touch her. Yet she needed to be touched. Held. Comforted—and loved…

Dear God. What am I saying? What am I thinking?

She kept her voice expressionless. 'He didn't mean it. He just wanted someone to work on the house for him and keep costs down. He didn't love me—and he didn't want to make love to me either. I see that now.'

'Then we're both marginally wiser than we were an hour ago.' Chay flung off the tangled sheet and swung himself off the bed, causing Adrien to look away hastily. Nothing was ever going to erase the memory of his body, naked against hers, but she didn't need any visual reminders to go with it.

He disappeared into the bathroom, reappearing a few minutes later tying the belt of a white towelling robe.

He said, 'I'm running you a bath. How badly did I hurt you?'

She tried to smile. 'I'll live.' She paused, her eyes searching his face. 'Chay—it had to happen some time. It's—not important.'

'There we disagree.' He bent and picked up the crumpled peignoir. 'I was right when I said you looked like a bride.' The grey eyes were chilly. 'I presume you bought this for Piers?'

'Yes.' Adrien lifted her chin. 'But I wore it for you.'

'Strange.' His mouth twisted. 'I only remember you taking it off. I'll go and check your bath.'

'I don't need a bath,' she said. 'But I'd really like to sleep for a while.'

'If that's what you want.' He put the peignoir down on the bed beside her. 'You'd better put this on.'

'To sleep in?' She was bewildered.

'No,' he said. 'To wear back to your own room.'

She stared at him, her heart beating a little faster as she huddled the peignoir around her. 'You—you don't want me to stay here?'

His smile was wintry. 'I think enough damage has been done already—don't you? Besides, virgin sacrifices have never been to my taste.' He tied the ribbons for her, his fingers impersonal, almost brisk. 'So it's best if you leave the Grange tomorrow.'

She sat very still, staring up at him. 'But—but Chay...' Her voice trembled into silence as she tried to find the right words.

His brows lifted. 'You're concerned you won't be paid if I go back on our deal?'

No, she thought blankly, that hadn't even entered her mind. Her attempt at protest had been on far more complex grounds, which she was still struggling to understand. Which she was frightened to face.

She lifted her chin. 'Of course,' she said. 'What else?'

'Well, don't worry, darling.' His tone was almost casual. 'You'll get your money.'

If he'd slapped her face she couldn't have felt more hurt, or more humiliated. She'd expected reassurance, and instead she was faced with rejection.

Piers hadn't wanted her, she thought numbly. And now Chay was turning her away too. And suddenly—for some unfathomable reason—she felt as if she was dying inside.

Dear God, she thought, swallowing. What's happening to me?

But she couldn't think about that now. Because the important thing—indeed, the only thing—was to get out of this room somehow, with what little remained of her pride. Before she said something—made some plea—that she would regret bitterly later. Or even broke down and cried like a baby.

He mustn't know how I feel, she thought. He must never find out.

From some hidden store of courage she conjured up a smile, and she rose to her feet and straightened her shoulders.

'Thank you,' she said, lightly. 'Somehow that makes it all—almost—worthwhile.'

And she walked to the door and went out, without looking back.

CHAPTER EIGHT

ADRIEN walked slowly and steadily to her room, but once the door was closed behind her she collapsed against it, gasping for breath as if she'd just run a marathon.

The pressure of the past week had got to her at last, and she'd gone slightly crazy. That was the only feasible explanation.

She could rationalise until she was blue in the face. She could come up with a whole range of excuses. But the truth was she'd gone to Chay tonight because she'd wanted him. And not just with her body, she admitted bleakly. Her heart and mind had surrendered too.

Even reliving the childhood trauma he'd inflicted on her hadn't deflected her even for a minute.

I was never able to remember it before, she thought wonderingly. Not in its entirety. I didn't want to examine the pain he'd caused too closely.

So why did I choose to do it—tonight of all nights? Why did I torture myself all over again? It makes no sense.

Yet even with all those memories—all that cause to hate him—she'd gone to him. Offered herself and been taken.

And then sent away.

And that, she thought, was the ultimate act of cruelty. None of the other things he'd done to her even came close.

It was pointless to remind herself that she was now free to leave. That, in essence, she'd beaten him. Because if this was victory, she never wanted to face defeat.

She stripped off the peignoir and threw it, rolled into a ball, to the back of the wardrobe. She never wanted to see it again. Tomorrow it would go in the firebox of the Aga.

Her body felt alien. She was wearing the scent of his skin, and if she was ever to close her eyes in peace again she had to rid herself of it. Along with some even more potent memories.

She'd allowed herself to be haunted by the past for far too long already. Now she would have the remembrance of Chay's hands touching her, the heat of his mouth on her eager flesh, to colour her dreams and twist her waking hours into helpless longing.

She hadn't known it was possible to want someone so badly, she realised. And telling herself that she was just a chronic case of sexual frustration, that any man would have done, was simply self-deception.

Because Chay had always been part of her life. He'd been her friend, her enemy, and, tonight, her lover.

It was as if every moment in her existence had been preparing her—leading her up to this. And now it was over.

She stood under the shower, using a body scrub until every inch of her tingled. She towelled herself dry, then put on the old jade bathrobe. Comfort-dressing, she thought, her mouth twisting.

She felt too restless to go to bed, and curled up in the armchair, tucking her feet under her, breathing in the faint drift of fragrance from the roses. Trying to calm herself. To make some kind of plan.

Her future was settled, she reminded herself. She had her home. The business was safe now, and they could continue to build on their success. And that was what she'd wanted to achieve.

But she'd had to pay an agonising price for her new-found security.

And now she had to consider her future peace of mind, with Chay living almost on her doorstep.

Avoiding the Grange physically shouldn't be too difficult, she thought determinedly. True, it stood on the main road out of the village, but there were other routes—slight detours—which she could take, especially at weekends when Chay would be there.

That wasn't the problem.

Somehow she had to accept it was no longer part of her life. That everything that had happened to her under its roof, and the man who was responsible for it, belonged to the past.

And could not be allowed to matter.

Or she would spend her life thinking of all the 'might have beens'. Which would be intolerable. Unbearable.

She repeated, 'Unbearable,' and only realised she'd spoken aloud when she heard the note of utter desolation in her own voice.

She eventually fell asleep towards dawn, and woke, cold and cramped, to the splash of rain against the window.

My God, she thought, catching sight of her little carriage clock. It's nearly ten o'clock.

She dressed hastily, flinging on a black knee-length skirt and a matching long-sleeved blouse, and ran downstairs.

'I'm sorry I'm so late,' she apologised, encountering Mrs Whitley in the hall.

'Mr Haddon said you were to have your sleep out, madam.' Mrs Whitley's eyes were shrewd, assessing Adrien's pale face and heavy eyes. 'What may I get you for breakfast?'

'I—I'm not hungry. Just some coffee, please.' Adrien hesitated. 'Where is Mr Haddon?'

'He went out first thing, madam. And he didn't say when he'd be back.' Mrs Whitley sounded disapproving. 'I'll bring your coffee to the dining room.'

When she did so, Adrien wasn't surprised to find it accompanied by a plate of creamy scrambled eggs and some crisp toast, which she ate obediently because it was marginally less trouble than arguing.

When she'd finished, she got up from the table and wandered to the window, standing irresolute as she watched the driving rain.

'Such a nasty day,' said Mrs Whitley, bustling in to clear the table. 'I hope the weather improves next weekend for Mr Haddon's visitors.'

'He's expecting guests?' Adrien turned, surprised.

'Oh, yes, madam. Some business acquaintances, I understand. It's been planned for some time. When Mr Haddon gives you the final list, we can decide on bedrooms and menus.' She nodded happily, as if she'd just bestowed a longed-for treat, and disappeared.

I should have told her, Adrien thought with a sigh, returning to her contemplation of the rain. I should have warned her that I won't be here.

Not that it really mattered, of course, she added drearily. Mrs Whitley could cope with a whole houseful of people with one hand tied behind her back.

And I, she thought, squaring her shoulders, I shall be living my own life again. And, as it can't start soon enough, I'll begin my packing right now.

She'd no idea what she was going to say to Zelda, of course, she mused as she went towards the stairs. Some carefully edited approximation of the truth, perhaps. After which the subject would be taboo.

A loud peal from the front doorbell halted her in her tracks. She called, 'It's all right, Mrs Whitley. I'll get it.'

There was a furniture lorry parked on the drive, and a man in waterproofs beaming at her. 'Nice to see you, Miss Lander. I've brought your bed.'

For a moment she stared at him uncomprehendingly, then realisation hit her like a brick.

'Oh, God,' she said. 'The four-poster. I—I'd forgotten all about it.'

That was what had been nagging at her all week, she thought. The bed she'd bought all those weeks ago for Piers and herself. Which Fred Derwent had now restored and was now trying to deliver. Which she'd forgotten to cancel.

She forced a smile. 'Fred—I should have contacted you. There's been a change of plan, I'm afraid. The Grange has been sold, and the new owner doesn't want a four-poster bed, so I'd like you to sell it for me—in your showroom.'

Fred's ruddy face drooped. 'Well, that's a pity. It's a fine bed, and I've made a good job of it, if I do say so myself. Is the gentleman sure he doesn't want it?'

'Absolutely certain.' She looked at him beseechingly. 'Fred, you'll have no trouble selling it—'

'Selling what?' Chay's voice interrupted brusquely. He'd arrived unnoticed from round the corner of the house, and was standing on the gravel, hands thrust into the pockets of his trench coat.

Fred Derwent turned to him eagerly. 'A beautiful four-poster bed, sir. A genuine antique that Miss Lander found and meant for this house. For the master bedroom, I understand. And if you're the new master that makes it yours, I reckon,' he added with a chuckle.

Chay's eyes rested dispassionately on Adrien, framed in the doorway, her face flushed, her eyes wide with trouble.

There was a pause, then he said, 'Of course. Will you bring it in, please? Perhaps your men could move the existing bed up to the attics?'

'Glad to, sir,' Fred said heartily. 'You've made the right decision.'

Chay's smile did not reach his eyes. 'I'll take your word for it Mr—er—Derwent,' he added, glancing at the side of the lorry. 'Now, let's get out of this rain. I'll ask my house-keeper to make us all some coffee.'

As he walked past Adrien her hand closed on his arm, halting him. Mr Derwent had returned to his lorry to superintend the unloading, and there was no one to overhear as she said quietly, urgently, 'Chay, you don't want it. You can't...'

His brows lifted. 'Why not? Because you planned to consummate your passion for Piers in it?' He shook his head, almost scornfully. 'That won't disturb my dreams, Adrien.'

Her hand dropped to her side. 'Then there's nothing more to be said.'

'Now there I disagree.' His tone was cool and brisk. 'Come to the library in fifteen minutes, will you? And tell Jean about the coffee, please. I'm going to change out of these wet things.'

It was the voice of a man who was used to being obeyed giving orders to a junior employee, Adrien realised furiously, finding herself trailing off obediently in search of Mrs Whitley. Not someone who'd held her naked in passion the previous night.

Apparently he was even readier to forget the whole disastrous episode than she was herself.

Well, that's good, she thought defiantly. Excellent, in fact.

She supposed he wanted to give her some kind of formal notice, or to finalise any outstanding payment arrangements.

Well, that was all right too. If she tried she could be out of the Grange before lunch.

She spoke to Mrs Whitley, then went up to her room and began dragging things out of the wardrobe and tossing them into her case, closing her ears to the sounds, at the other end of the corridor, of a four-poster bed being brought upstairs and assembled.

When fifteen minutes had elapsed, she went down to the library and knocked at the door.

Chay's 'Come in' held a note of weary exasperation.

He was seated behind Angus Stretton's big desk, scanning through the morning's mail delivery, and as he looked up Adrien checked, her hand going to her throat.

The firm mouth tightened. 'Good God, Adie, I can't have startled you this time,' he rasped. 'You knew I was here.'

'I'm sorry.' She steadied herself. 'It's just—seeing you there, where Angus always sat. For a moment I felt as if I were seeing a ghost.'

He glanced back at the letter he was reading. 'I didn't know the Grange was supposed to be haunted.' He sounded coolly indifferent.

'It's not,' she said. 'And that's not what I meant...'

'Ah, yes,' he said. 'I have no real right to be in this house, or at this desk, and if there was any justice I'd be serving a life sentence without remission for traumatising your childhood and stealing from you on your eighteenth birthday.' He delivered the words with stinging contempt. 'Isn't that the way it goes?'

She bit her lip. 'Believe it or not, I didn't mean that either. I—I came to tell you that I'm ready to leave within the hour. If that's all right.'

He put the letter he was holding down on the desk, crumpling the envelope and tossing it into the waste basket. Then he looked at her, the grey eyes expressionless.

He said, 'Take a seat, Adie. I think we need to talk.'

She remained standing. 'Everything necessary was said last night. You said I should leave.'

'And now I'm asking you to work a month's notice.'

'I'm sorry,' she said. 'I'm afraid the terms of employment are unacceptable.'

'I suppose that's a reference to last night's sexual fiasco,' he said softly. 'However, as I've already indicated, I can safely promise there'll be no repetition of that.'

He paused. Then, 'I think Jean told you I'm having people to stay next weekend. These are men I do business with, and their wives. I need a lady of my own to meet them, and act as my hostess. I'd like you to do this for me.'

'Give me one good reason why I should.'

He said gently, 'I could mention thousands. But I'd like to think you were generous enough to help me out here.'

'Make it a week's notice,' she said. 'And I'll consider it.'

Chay shook his head. 'It has to be a month. That's not negotiable.'

'But why? I want to get on with my life.'

'And I want to ensure that you can.' He paused again. 'Tell me, Adie, are you on the Pill?'

Her brows snapped together. 'Of course not—' she began, then halted, her lips parted in sheer consternation as she met his sardonic gaze. She said, 'No—it's not possible. It can't be...'

Suddenly she needed to sit down. She groped for the chair he'd indicated and sank on to it.

Chay shrugged. 'We had unprotected sex, Adrien. Again, I hadn't bargained for your extreme state of innocence,' he added drily. 'I thought if you were sleeping with Mendoza, you'd be geared up accordingly.'

'How—dare you?'

His mouth twisted. 'It was an honest mistake, Adie. I only wish you'd been equally candid.' He allowed her to digest that for a second, then went on, 'But, as you can see, I have good reason for keeping you here until I can be sure I haven't made you pregnant.'

'If I am,' she said, 'it'll be my problem, and I'll deal with it.'

'No,' he said. 'It concerns me too, so cool the display of fighting spirit.' He sent her a mocking glance. 'I know you have red hair, Adrien. You don't need to keep demonstrating the fact.'

She glared at him. 'My hair is auburn,' she began, and then realised she'd fallen right into his trap. Remembered with heart-stopping clarity how he'd used to call her 'Ginger' and 'Carrots' all those years before, winding her up until she launched herself at him in fury.

She saw his mouth soften into a grin of pure appreciation, and found, astonished, that she was smiling reluctantly in response.

She said, 'You brute.'

'Well, that's almost a term of endearment compared with some of the names you've called me recently.' He leaned back in his chair, watching her from under his lids. 'So—are you going to stay, Adie? Naturally, I don't want to pressure you...'

'But you will if you have to,' she supplied bitterly.

'Perhaps,' he said. 'But I'd rather you agreed of your own accord. Is it really so much to ask?'

More than you can ever know. The thought swam into her mind, and was instantly banished.

She looked down at her tightly clasped hands. 'I—suppose not. And, anyway, you'll only be around at weekends.'

Oh, God, she thought immediately. Why did I say that?

Glancing apprehensively at Chay, she saw his face harden.

'I shall be here,' he said, his voice biting, 'just as often as the mood takes me. This is now my home, and I'm not staying away to spare your feelings, Adrien. However, I'll take your response as grudging consent.'

He paused. 'After all, I now have an extra bill to pay—for the bed you so conveniently forgot about.'

She said in a stifled voice, 'You didn't have to keep it. I was quite prepared to send it back.'

'You were positively eager to do so.' His mouth curled. 'Poor Adrien. Did it revive too many unhappy memories?'

'It didn't revive any memories at all,' she said. 'As you know.'

Again, she wished the last words unsaid as soon as she'd spoken, but he only nodded.

He got to his feet and walked round the desk, standing looking down at her, his expression unreadable.

He said quietly, 'Are you all right, Adie?'

Colour warmed her face. 'I'm fine,' she said quickly. 'Now, can we forget about it, please?'

His mouth twisted without humour. 'You can, I'm sure. I shan't find it quite so easy.'

He allowed the words to die into a tingling silence, then reached behind him and picked up a sheet of paper from the desk. 'Is this your work?'

'Yes,' Adrien said, swallowing, glad to move to the impersonal. 'It's something I was working on yesterday—a plan for the kitchen garden. I shouldn't have left it around.'

'It's good,' he said. 'When the contractors arrive next week, I'd like you to show it to them—get them to work on it.'

'The kitchen garden's a long-term project,' Adrien said hastily, getting to her feet. 'I—I really shouldn't get involved.'

He gave her a swift, wry smile. 'But you already are involved, Adrien,' he said softly. 'You know it, and so do I.' He went back to his chair and picked up another envelope. 'I'll see you at lunch,' he added casually.

Adrien closed the library door behind her and took a deep breath. It seemed, in spite of everything, she'd committed herself to another month under Chay's roof. Four weeks, she thought. Hardly a lifetime. Unless...

For a moment her hand strayed tentatively to her abdomen.

No, she told herself with determination. It's not true. *It can't be true.*

But, at the same time, she wouldn't have a quiet moment until she finally learned the truth. And maybe not then, she reminded herself painfully, and went slowly back upstairs to take her clothes out of the case.

As she reached the head of the stairs, Fred Derwent hailed her cheerfully. 'Your bed looks wonderful, Miss Lander. This room really sets it off.'

'Oh—good.' Adrien gave him a fleeting smile and turned towards her own room, but he was not to be gainsaid.

'Come and have a look,' he urged.

Reluctantly, she walked to Chay's bedroom doorway and peeped in. Mrs Whitley was there, busying herself with sheets and pillowcases.

'Beautiful, isn't it?' She ran an approving hand over one of the carved posts. 'What it really needs, of course, is curtains, and one of those canopy things.'

'They'll be coming,' Mr Derwent assured her. 'Miss Lander's partner was making them special. Isn't that right?'

Aware of their expectant glances, Adrien nodded feebly.

'When will they be ready?' Mrs Whitley asked eagerly.

'They—they're already finished,' Adrien admitted. 'I—could go and fetch them.'

'That would be wonderful.' Mrs Whitley beamed. 'The exact finishing touch.'

'Then I'll go now.' Adrien glanced at her watch. 'Would you tell Mr Haddon I won't be here for lunch, please?'

The rain had stopped and a watery sun had broken through the clouds when she arrived at the cottage.

She'd been gone for less than twenty-four hours, but already the cottage had an oddly disused air about it.

Only a month, Adrien comforted herself. And then it will belong to me again. And I'll come over as often as possible. Put fresh flowers around. Open the windows.

She collected her post, listed the messages on the answering machine, and made herself some coffee to drink with the ham roll she'd bought at the village shop.

Then she locked up, and walked across the courtyard to Zelda's flat.

Zelda opened the door to her knock. 'Hi.' Her voice was surprised. 'I didn't expect to see you today.'

Adrien smiled constrainedly. 'I thought I'd come and collect the curtains and canopy that you made for the four-poster bed. It—arrived today.'

Zelda stared at her. 'Didn't you cancel it?'

Adrien bit her lip. 'I forgot.'

Zelda's face broke into a grin. 'I think that's what they call a Freudian slip.'

'Nothing of the kind,' Adrien said with a faint snap. 'I just had other things on my mind. Now, may I have the keys to the workroom, please?'

Zelda went with her, and helped her load the heavy bundles of fabric into the Jeep.

She said, frowningly, 'Are you all right?'

'Fine. Never better,' Adrien lied. She nodded. 'It's all going really well.'

'Really?' Zelda gave her a measuring look. 'Why don't I come back with you and help you hang these things? You know how you are with ladders.'

'Not any more,' Adrien said briskly. 'I've put all that nonsense behind me now.'

'Then let me come for moral support.'

Adrien climbed into the Jeep. 'Isn't this the day Smudge gets his puppy?'

'That could wait till tomorrow.'

Adrien shook her head. 'No,' she said. 'He's waited quite long enough. I'll be over to see you all very soon.'

'One day,' Zelda said grimly, 'I expect you to tell me exactly what's going on.'

I wish I knew myself, Adrien thought, as she put the Jeep in gear and drove off with a cheerful wave.

The Grange seemed deserted when she got back. It took several trips to take the bulky material up to Chay's room, and then she had to search the outbuildings for a pair of suitable steps.

Not too high, she reassured herself as she carried them upstairs. Start in a small way, and build on that, and you'll be fine.

With her bottom lip caught in her teeth, she climbed up carefully, the swathe of fabric over her shoulder.

'Don't look down,' she muttered under her breath. 'Just don't look down.'

Ten minutes later she was wondering what had made her think this was a job for one pair of hands. Despite her best efforts, the heavy canopy refused to stay in place while she fixed the corners.

'Damn the thing,' she muttered, leaning over further to tug it straight, only to feel the steps begin to wobble as the balance of her weight altered.

She gave a little cry, and clutched at the nearest bedpost to steady herself.

And heard Chay's voice say grimly, 'What the hell do you think you're doing?'

She looked down and saw him beside her. Below her, looking up. And suddenly the old nightmare took possession again, and the green carpet was grass, and she was a terrified child, realising how far she could fall.

'Don't touch me.' Her voice rose hysterically. 'Don't touch the ladder.'

He said grimly, 'Don't be a fool, Adie. I've got you. Down you come.'

'No.' As his hands gripped her waist she kicked out at him.

Chay swore, lifting her away from the steps, turning her

in his arms so that she was pinned against him, her breasts crushed against the wall of his chest, her dilated eyes staring into his. Holding her there until she stopped struggling and the small dry sobs died away, leaving only the hurry of their breathing to disturb the tense silence.

He said harshly, 'You just don't get it, do you, Adie?'

Then, infinitely slowly, he began to lower her to the ground, still watching her, letting every inch of her body linger tellingly against his.

She felt the first dark shiver of arousal ripple through her. Heard herself whimper softly as her head fell back and her lips parted, inviting his kiss.

Then, abruptly, there was the quick tap of approaching footsteps, a gasp and a murmured apology, and Adrien turned her head to see Mrs Whitley beating an embarrassed retreat.

Chay said, 'Jean—wait a minute.' He set Adrien gently and unhurriedly down on the floor, then turned to the housekeeper hesitating in the doorway.

He said, 'Jean, you can hang these curtains, please?' He paused, adding silkily, 'Miss Lander has no head for heights.'

He divided a swift, impersonal smile between the pair of them, and walked out of the room.

Mrs Whitley came forward, tutting. 'You should have come to me, madam,' she said reproachfully. 'Why, you're as white as a sheet.'

'I thought I'd fall,' Adrien said, half to herself, still staring at the door. Still seeing the image of Chay walking away from her, with that long lithe stride that she knew so well. It wasn't the first time, she thought, so why should she suddenly find it so disturbing?'

'Then I'll stand on the steps and you can hand everything up to me,' Mrs Whitley said firmly. She stroked the material. 'Such lovely colours—and beautiful workmanship.'

She chatted quietly and inconsequentially as the curtains were hung round the bed and at the tall windows, and while the canopy was adjusted, and Adrien replied at random, her thoughts whirling as she tried to rationalise the feeling of unease which Chay's abrupt departure had triggered.

When everything was finished, and admired, and Mrs Whitley had disappeared to restore the steps to their usual place, Adrien escaped to her room. She curled up on the window seat, looking down at the sodden garden.

She'd given herself a fright, but it was over now, and anyway, Chay had been there to rescue her. Just as he had been all those years before, guiding her down from the treehouse, she recalled. Trying to make belated amends, she had supposed bitterly, for stranding her there. Or pretending that he hadn't been the one to do it, not knowing that she'd looked down and seen him—walking away.

Except—except that it was all wrong, she realised, frowning. The figure walking away from her, imprinted in her mind, had had a much shorter stride. Had held himself differently. Hadn't been as tall.

She thought, with a kind of anguish, I know Chay. I know everything about him and I always have. I've carried that knowledge with me all these years, no matter how it hurt. So how could I not have seen that it wasn't him at all—but someone wearing his grey jacket?

It had to have been Piers, of course, she recognised with an odd calm. Piers—the Grange's future owner—who had resented Chay as an interloper. Piers, who'd deliberately smashed Chay's field glasses and had been determined to wreck his private sanctuary too. Who had wanted Chay blamed and sent away.

But why? she asked herself in bewilderment. Why such an extreme reaction over the housekeeper's son?

'You don't get it,' Chay had said to her.

But I do now, she thought. I know exactly how it happened.

And maybe Chay himself could tell her why.

She had to find him, explain to him the self-deception she'd been practising all this time. And ask him—somehow—to forgive her.

And there was no time like the present, she thought, steeling herself as she got up from the window seat.

She ran lightly downstairs, not giving herself time for second thoughts, and tapped on the library door. There was no reply, and she knocked again more loudly.

'Miss Lander?' Mrs Whitley spoke from behind her. 'I was just coming to tell you that I've put some tea for you in the drawing room.'

'Oh, thank you,' Adrien hesitated. 'Has Mr Haddon gone out again?'

'Yes, madam.' Mrs Whitley's pleasant face took on a faintly wooden look. 'Unfortunately, he's had to go back to London. He asked me to make his apologies and say he'll see you next weekend.'

'When his guests are expected,' Adrien said quietly.
'Yes, of course.' She mustered a smile. 'Thank you, Mrs Whitley.'

The tea looked delicious. Tiny triangular sandwiches, a sponge filled with jam and cream, and a plate of home-made biscuits. But Adrien could not have eaten a crumb.

Because Chay had not simply walked away. He'd walked out.

She thought, in desolation, I've left it too late—and now he's gone. I've lost him. And tasted tears, hot and scalding, in her throat.

CHAPTER NINE

'IF WE'RE not careful,' Zelda said gleefully. 'We're going to have a full order book.'

'Seems like it,' Adrien agreed, brows furrowed as she checked an estimate. 'What's caused this sudden flurry of activity?'

'Christmas cards in the shops,' Zelda told her solemnly. 'People realise that, although it's only September, the countdown to hell has started, and they want to rethink the decor in their houses before the relations start arriving.'

She paused. 'At least there isn't that problem at the Grange. I hope Chay's guests will be duly impressed.'

'So do I,' Adrien said drily. 'But I doubt it. They all seem pretty high-powered.' She sighed. 'Chay's PA has faxed me details of all their interests and likes and dislikes, so that I can plan their entertainment with more precision.'

'Ouch,' said Zelda. 'Rather you than me.'

'Oh, it's not too onerous.' Adrien slid the estimate into an envelope and sealed it. 'The men want to play golf, which is easy. As for the wives, one of them is mad about tennis, another likes to swim, and the third collects antiques. So I've arranged temporary membership of the Country Club for the entire weekend, and a visit to the antiques fair at Lower Winkleigh on Sunday morning.'

She frowned slightly. 'On Saturday evening some of the local people have been invited to a drinks party.'

'Anyone interesting?'

'Sally Parfitt sent out the invitations from the London office some time ago. They're mostly the older generation,

I think. People who knew Angus Stretton.' Her frown deepened. 'Which is odd, really.'

'Or a shrewd move. Wooing the people who matter?' Zelda suggested. She put down the book of fabric samples she'd been examining. 'Anyway, I hope the master of the house appreciates your efforts. When does he plan to return?'

Adrien shrugged. 'Around lunchtime tomorrow, I suppose,' she said neutrally. 'The guests will be arriving during the afternoon, and he'll want to be there to welcome them.' She hesitated. 'I feel as if I'm leaving you in the lurch, now that all this work has started to come in. But it won't be for much longer.'

Zelda sent her a half-smile. 'I'll take your word for it, honey.'

Adrien picked up the pile of envelopes from the desk. 'I'll take these to the post, then get back. I have to sort out something to wear at dinner tomorrow evening.' She pulled a face. 'I'm not expected to compete, so I guess my all-purpose black will do.'

'I'd like to think it had some purpose,' Zelda said, and dodged, laughing, as Adrien threw a ball of crumpled paper at her.

Out in the courtyard, Smudge was playing with his puppy, an eager, bright-eyed bundle with ominously large paws, whom Zelda had christened Bugsy Malone in tribute, she said, to his criminal tendencies.

Smudge was a different kid these days, Adrien thought, pausing to watch them affectionately. So perhaps some good had come out of the past fraught few weeks after all.

She'd waited the rest of last weekend, hoping for a message of some kind from Chay, explaining his abrupt departure. But there'd been nothing. And the only contact this week had been through his PA.

'Adie—watch.' Smudge had spotted her. 'Bugsy can do a trick. He can roll over.'

Adrien hid a smile as the puppy lay on his back, waving his paws in the air. 'Wow,' she said, crouching down to tickle the velvety tummy with a gentle hand. 'He's a very intelligent dog.'

'He's got to have injections,' Smudge said. 'I can take him for walks. Will you come too, Adie?'

'Whenever I can,' Adrien told him, rising to her feet again.

'You live at the Grange now,' Smudge persisted. 'Why do you? I liked it when you lived in the cottage. When are you coming back? I miss you.' He put his arms round her and buried his face in her skirt.

Adrien touched his hair. 'I miss you, too. And I'll be coming back very soon.'

She heard a slight sound, and looked up. Chay was standing a few yards away, watching her, his expression cold and bleak.

She said, aware that her pulses had begun to behave erratically, 'What are you doing here? You're a day early...'

'You weren't at the house,' he said. 'I came to make sure you hadn't run out on me.'

Adrien gently detached Smudge's clinging hands. 'You said I could continue with my business,' she reminded him. 'It won't manage itself.'

'I haven't forgotten. However, this weekend is important to me, and your primary role is as my hostess.'

'You've bought my services,' she said. 'And you won't be short-changed. I think you'll find everything in place.'

'I hope so.'

Oh, why are we sniping at each other? she asked herself in anguish. This isn't how I planned it at all.

But then Chay's unexpected arrival had wrong-footed her completely.

'Are you going with that man?' Smudge suddenly demanded.

'I have to,' she told him. 'He's my boss.'

Smudge turned a mutinous look on Chay. 'Why can't you leave Adie alone?'

'Because I need her,' Chay said. 'To work for me.'

'When she's finished work, can she come back here?'

'I think,' Chay said quietly, 'we'll have to wait and see.' He looked at Adrien. 'Are you going straight to the Grange?'

'I have to go to the post office first.' Adrien waved to Smudge as she turned away.

'Then I'll walk with you.' Chay fell into step beside her.

He looked tired, she thought. She wanted to kiss the tautness from his mouth and close his eyes with her fingertips. She wanted to hold him. To draw his head down to her breast and let him sleep.

The longing to touch him twisted inside her like a knife in a wound.

He said, his tone expressionless, 'You have an admirer.'

She forced a smile. 'He's a terrific kid. Things haven't been easy for him.'

'He was one of your concerns when you agreed to our arrangement.' It was a statement, not a question.

She bent her head. 'Yes.' There was a silence, then she said, 'Why did you come to look for me?'

'Just protecting my investment, darling.' His voice was light and cynical.

'You didn't need to come down today,' she said carefully. 'Mrs Whitley and I have everything under control.'

'You mean you'd find it more convenient if I only showed for a few hours at the weekends.' His tone hardened. 'The Grange is my home, Adie, and I'll visit it when I want.' He paused. 'And if that's a problem for you, then deal with it.'

'That isn't what I meant.' She bit her lip. 'Chay—let's not have any more misunderstandings. The weekend's going to be difficult enough without us being at each other's throats.'

'I thought everything was arranged.'

'Not that,' she said. 'I'm wondering how your guests will regard me. As I'm living in your house, they're bound to make assumptions.'

'Would you like me to wear a badge?' His tone bit. '"I am not sleeping with this woman"?'

'Now you're being ridiculous,' she said wearily. 'Just forget I said anything. And here's the post office.'

'Ah,' Chay said derisively. 'I thought it looked familiar. And across the road is a café. Why don't we share a civilised pot of tea together while we figure a way to lessen your embarrassment?'

'"Civilised",' she said, pushing her envelopes into the mailbox, 'is hardly a word I'd use to describe our relationship.'

His mouth twisted into a smile. 'Maybe you bring out the barbarian in me, Adie. But I want this weekend to be relaxed, and it won't be if you're seething with resentment.'

'Perhaps you could refer to me as another PA, like Sally Parfitt,' she suggested. 'Let me maintain a low profile.'

They halted in front of the café, and Chay's hand closed on her shoulder, turning her slightly so that she could see her reflection in the plate glass window.

He said harshly, 'Take a good look at yourself, Adrien. Look at your hair, your skin, your eyes. You couldn't fade into the background if you tried. And it would fool no one anyway.'

'Why not?'

'Because of this,' he said. And pulled her towards him. The kiss was brief, but searingly, hungrily explicit in its demand. He didn't use any force, but when he let her go

Adrien had the absurd impression that her lips were bruised.

She took a step backwards, fighting the insidious throb of excitement which made her want to go back into his arms. Offer her mouth again. She stared up at him, searching for something to say, trying to read his expression. But the grey eyes were hooded.

He said laconically, 'Now we've given the gossips a field-day, let's have that tea.'

She ought to refuse. She *wanted* to refuse. To make some excuse, find the Jeep and drive somewhere that he'd never find her again.

Yet somehow they were in the café, and Chay was ordering tea and a plate of sandwiches.

'Jean says you don't eat enough,' he remarked, as the young waitress departed.

'I'm perfectly all right,' she retorted. 'Jean fusses too much.'

'I think I'll let you tell her that yourself.'

He sounded coolly friendly, she realised with wonder. As if that sudden blaze of desire had never existed.

She took a deep breath. 'Chay—I need to talk to you about something.'

'Are you quite sure it's necessary?' His gaze met hers levelly.

She swallowed. 'It's important—to me.'

'Are you going to tell me you're pregnant?'

'Of course not. It's far too soon to know.'

'There are tests—aren't there?' The question was casually interested.

'Yes,' she said. 'But I don't need one. There's no baby.'

'How can you be sure?'

Because I'd know, she thought. Because your child would be a beautiful glowing secret to be sheltered inside me. And instead I just feel—empty.

She said shortly, 'Female intuition.'

His mouth curled. 'Not the most reliable monitor.'

She supposed it was a reference to Piers, and bit her lip.

At that point the tea arrived, and setting out the crockery and pouring the tea provided a brief diversion.

As she passed him his cup, she said, 'You're probably right. Mine's been letting me down for years.' She paused. 'Why didn't you tell me that it was Piers who stranded me in the treehouse and not you?'

'Because it was easier that way,' he said after a pause. His hand strayed to the scar on his cheekbone. 'Or it was before you started using me as target practice.'

'But you were sent away,' she said soberly. 'It must have been dreadful for you. And it wrecked your relationship with Angus. You were rarely allowed back to the Grange after that, even in vacations.'

'And when I did return there was more trouble. Is that what you're leading up to?'

She winced. 'I'm trying to understand,' she said. 'I can see how angry you must have been. How bitter.'

And when Angus rejected you again it must have been the last straw, she thought. You wanted to hit out—and there I was—being indulged by Angus and given expensive presents. You wanted to punish me for my part in it all.

'I was exiled to the sixth form in one of the best schools in the country, and then on to university,' Chay told her drily. He offered her the sandwiches and took one himself. 'Hardly penal servitude.'

'Oh,' she said, remembering that overheard conversation between her parents. 'But I thought...'

'I know what you thought,' he said. 'And what you still think, for that matter. What's this all about, Adie?'

Adrien looked down at the tablecloth. 'I thought it was time I apologised for my part in it all.'

'Consider it done.' He sounded indifferent. 'It was all a long time ago.'

'But still having repercussions—in both our lives,' she said in a low voice. 'Isn't that why you bought the Grange?'

'Yes.' His tone was suddenly uncompromising. 'I always intended it to belong to me.'

She swallowed. 'And—was I part of the plan?'

'Yes.' His smile was crooked. 'Which just proves how unwise some ambitions can be.' He paused. 'I've got something to tell you, too, Adrien.'

He was going to confess that he'd stolen the pendant, she thought wretchedly. And she couldn't bear it. Because nothing could excuse the damage he'd done to Angus and to herself, and she couldn't face hearing him admit that he was capable of inflicting that kind of hurt.

She glanced at her watch and manufactured an exclamation. 'I've got an appointment with a client. She's got this very dark dining room... So, I—I'll see you back at the house later.'

She saw his face close, and a sudden bleakness enter the grey eyes. He said quietly, rising to his feet, 'As you wish.'

Adrien sent him a swift, meaningless smile and fled.

She drove out of the village, deliberately choosing a road that would take her in the opposite direction to the Grange. She needed to distance herself so that she could sort out the turmoil in her mind.

She parked in a lay-by and leaned back in her seat, closing her eyes, letting her memory pick its way painfully back across the years.

She'd been touched and surprised when Angus Stretton had said he was giving a party for her at the Grange to celebrate her eighteenth birthday.

'I always wanted a daughter to spoil,' he told her. 'And it's kind of your parents to allow me to share this special time with you all.' He smiled at her kindly. 'And it's time this house was livened up.'

Adrien thought what a shame it was that he didn't have a family living with him at the Grange. Guarded remarks from her parents had told her that Mr Stretton was married, but his wife was an invalid, permanently confined to a nursing home.

But it was good that he had Piers, she told herself. And even better that Piers would be paying one of his periodic visits that weekend of her party. None of her friends had met him, and with his dark good looks he was going to cause a sensation.

But she didn't expect Chay to be there.

It had been two years since she'd seen him. And before that she'd gone out of her way to avoid him, staying away from the Grange altogether during his brief sojourns.

But when he'd smiled at her, and said her name, she'd found it difficult to maintain her hostility.

Besides, that tall, cool-eyed stranger had borne no resemblance to the quiet boy who'd turned from friend to enemy. And who seemed to want to be her friend again.

And when he'd said gently, 'Adie—am I still the monster from your childhood?' she'd forgotten she was sixteen and officially an adult, and had blushed to the roots of her hair, stammering some disclaimer.

Within a day he'd been gone again, but Adrien had found their fleeting encounter impossible to put out of her mind. His image seemed lodged in her head, waking or sleeping.

Looking back, she could see there had hardly been a day when she hadn't thought about him. When she hadn't wondered where he was and what he was doing. And when he would return...

Slowly but surely, the memory of him had become implanted in her heart and mind and started to bloom.

So when she went up to the Grange on her birthday

morning, and found him standing there in the drawing room, she ran to him on a blaze of happiness which took her straight into his arms. And then his mouth touched hers, warm, sensuous and very assured. Making no concessions to her inexperience. Imposing a subtle demand that was totally new to her, and which scared and thrilled her in equal measure.

When at last he lifted his head, he said softly, 'Well, now...'

Then they heard Angus coming, with her father, and fell apart. Angus paused when he saw them, and glanced at Chay, his expression almost wary, and Chay looked back, smiling faintly.

Then they began to discuss the final arrangements for the party, and the odd little moment was forgotten.

'Isn't it wonderful that Chay's home?' she asked her father as they walked home.

'Not particularly,' he said shortly. 'Because it will mean that those never-ending demands for money will start all over again. And Angus deserves some peace.'

The dismissive words shocked her. Was that really why Chay had come back? she thought, feeling sick with disappointment. Because Angus was a rich man and Chay was trying to get a business of his own off the ground?

The question hung over her like a shadow all day, but it couldn't spoil the anticipation of her party. As well as her friends from school, a lot of the local people were going, and Angus had hired a disco and arranged a lavish buffet supper.

Adrien wore a cream silky dress, with the gold watch her parents had given her on her wrist and small gold studs in her ears.

She was desperate to see Chay, to feel his arms around her again and seek the reassurance she needed from his kiss, but he seemed to be keeping his distance. Everyone wanted to dance with the birthday girl, and Chay appeared content with that. Later, she told herself. Later she'd be alone with him and it would all be different.

She could feel the blood move in her veins, thick and sweet as honey. Could feel her skin tingle and warm in expectation of his touch.

He'd come back for her sake, she told herself. That was how it had to be.

Piers was much in evidence, of course, and Adrien told herself she didn't mind too badly, because he was a fantastic dancer and had murmured that she looked beautiful. And it might give Chay something to think about too.

Angus had already given her a collection of classical music on CD, but during the course of the evening he called for silence and presented her with a velvet jewellery box.

He said, 'For my wished-for daughter,' and smiled at her while everyone laughed and applauded.

When Adrien opened it she found a garnet pendant gleaming at her. The stones were set in a delicate oval of gold, and instinct told her that the piece was very old, and probably valuable. She gasped and stammered her thanks, and Chay lifted it gently from its satin bed and fastened it round her throat.

She felt the brush of his fingers on her nape and bent her head to hide the excited flush which warmed her face.

'The clasp doesn't seem terribly reliable,' he commented. 'You'd better be careful, Adie.'

Later those words would come back to haunt her.

Eventually, worried that the clasp might give way while she was dancing, she replaced the lovely thing in its box and put it with the rest of her presents in the library.

But when the party was over, and she went to collect her things, she couldn't resist having another look, and found the box empty.

She stood staring down at it, her brain going numb as

tendrils of fright began to uncurl inside her. Had she only imagined taking it off? she wondered frantically. Was it lying on the floor somewhere, broken?

'What's wrong, sweetheart?' Piers had entered the library behind her, and she mutely held out the empty case, her eyes enormous in her white face.

He said softly, 'So, we have a thief amongst us. My uncle has to know about this.'

He took her arm and marched her back to the drawing room.

'Adrien's pendant has been stolen,' he announced abruptly, indicating the empty case she was holding. 'I say the police should be called.'

I'm dreaming, Adrien thought. This is a nightmare, and soon I'll wake up and it will be over.

There was a brief and terrible silence. She could see her parents looking aghast, and Angus's face, stricken, suddenly old and defeated, as he turned to look at Chay.

He said tiredly, 'You'd better go and get it. I suppose it's in your room.'

And Chay said quietly, the grey eyes defiant, 'You know it is.'

Angus nodded. 'You'll fetch it,' he said. 'And then you'll leave this house and not come back. Or I can't answer for the consequences.'

'And that's it?' Piers demanded angrily. 'He comes back here scrounging, tries to steal from a guest under this roof, and you just let him go? I say he should be arrested.'

'You're not the master here yet, Piers.' Angus's voice was bitterly forceful. 'I will handle this matter as I wish. Chay will return the pendant to me, and then he'll leave.'

It was warm in the room, but Adrien felt cold and dizzy suddenly. She caught at her father's sleeve. 'Can we go—now—please? I can't bear any more.'

'Yes, of course,' he said swiftly. 'I'm sorry, darling.'

Her mother came to her side, putting a sympathetic arm round her, urging her out of the room.

Back at the cottage, she lay on her bed, uncaring of the creases in the cream dress.

She said, 'Why did he do it?'

Her father said quietly, 'Angus refused to give him any more money. That was his revenge. I'm only sorry that he chose to involve you. That was too cruel.' He paused. 'You'll get the pendant back, of course.'

'No.' Adrien began to cry, sobs shaking her body. 'No, I don't want to see it ever again. It's spoiled—all spoiled.'

It would always remind her of Chay, fastening it round her throat. Of his touch on her skin. And she never wanted to remember that—never.

Not just the party had been spoiled, she realised. But her whole life.

Because Chay, whom she loved, was a thief, and therefore lost to her for ever.

Adrien stirred, opening her eyes, forcing herself back to reality. For a moment, as she looked at the windscreen, she thought it was raining again. Until she realised that it was her own eyes that were blurred, her face wet with tears as all the old pain tore into her. As the sheer force of everything she felt for him overwhelmed her.

Her unfulfilled body was starving for him, craving him, but that was only part of it. Her heart and mind wanted him too, she thought, pressing a clenched fist to her trembling mouth. Needed him as fiercely as she needed air to breathe.

Had there ever been a time when she hadn't loved him? she asked herself. All these years she'd fought her longing for him, trying to hide behind barricades of bitterness and contempt. Hoping that if she told herself over and over again that she hated him, that would somehow make it true.

But she knew now that all her denials had been useless.

She thought with desperation, I loved him then, and I love him now. But I can't stay with a man I can't trust. And that's all there is to it.

And until he allows me to leave, I shall simply have to—endure.

And presently, when she had no more tears left, she started the engine and drove back to the Grange, to face the time that was left.

CHAPTER TEN

THANKFULLY, there was no one about when she got back to the Grange, and Adrien was able to whisk her tear-stained face and bedraggled appearance safely to her room.

She took a long shower, using her favourite scented gel, and shampooed her hair rigorously. She felt as if she was shedding the past like a skin. And if she kept her eyes firmly on the future, however bleak it might seem, she'd be able—somehow—to cope with the present. That was the theory, anyway. In practice, living under the same roof with Chay but not living with him, it might not be so easy.

She towelled herself dry and slipped on lacy briefs and a matching bra. Then, wrapped in the old jade robe, she curled up in her armchair and switched on her hairdryer, combing the long auburn strands with her fingers and flicking them into place with the deftness of long practice.

She had almost finished when a peremptory rap at her door cut across the buzz of the drier. She clicked the off switch and went to answer it, tightening the sash of her robe.

Chay was waiting with thinly veiled impatience. 'I thought you'd gone into purdah.' The grey eyes flicked over her. 'Didn't you hear me knocking?'

'I've been drying my hair.' Just the sight of him was enough to start that helpless inner trembling.

'So I see.' He reached out and fingered one silky strand. His mouth twisted slightly. 'You look about sixteen, Adie, do you know that?'

She thought, her face warming, And when you look at me like that, I feel sixteen again.

Aloud, she said with a certain constraint, 'Did you want something? Is there a problem?'

'I came to give you this.' He bent and retrieved a large flat box tied with ribbons that had been propped against the wall, and handed it to her.

'What is it?' Adrien looked at it uncertainly.

'Open it,' he advised, following her into the room.

She untied the ribbons, lifted the lid and parted the folds of tissue paper. The sheen of satin met her eyes. Black, she thought, until the light caught it and she saw a shimmer like deep crimson.

It was a dress, she realised as she lifted it out and held it up. Low-necked and long-sleeved, with a brief swirl of a skirt cut cleverly on the bias.

He said, 'I'd like you to wear it for the drinks party on Saturday.' He paused. 'They call it Venetian red.'

'It—it's beautiful.' Her mouth was dry. 'But you don't have to buy me clothes. That's not part of the deal.'

He shrugged. 'Look on it as a bonus for all the work you've done for this weekend.'

It was as if the deepest, darkest mahogany had suddenly become fluid, she thought, feeling the beguiling slide of the fabric through her fingers.

She said, 'How did you know my size?'

'Would you believe—instinct?'

Her lips trembled into a smile. 'That's probably as dangerous as female intuition.'

'I back my judgement,' he said.

'And the colour,' she went on. 'I—I never wear red.'

The grey eyes met hers. 'Try it on and see.'

He was still formally attired in the dark business suit he'd been wearing earlier. He walked across to the armchair and sat down, loosening the knot of his tie and unbuttoning the close-fitting waistcoat.

Her throat tightened. 'In front of you?'

He nodded. 'Here—and now.' He leaned back in the chair, stretching out long legs. 'I've decided to take you up on your previous offer,' he added softly.

She'd always known she would regret that particular piece of bravado. And he was waiting for her to protest— to remind him that theirs was a business relationship—that he'd promised...

Lifting her chin, Adrien untied the sash of her robe, letting her gaze meet his in direct challenge as she took it off and tossed it to the floor.

One glance at the dress's wide, deeply scooped neckline had already told her that she wouldn't be able to wear a bra under it.

Still watching him, she reached round and unfastened the clip, shrugging the narrow straps from her shoulders. For a moment she held it in front of her, using the lace cups as a shield, her hands deliberately teasing before she removed it altogether, letting it flow down to join her robe on the floor. She no longer felt awkward or shy under his intense scrutiny. She wanted him to look at her. To do more than look. To touch, and to take. As she would take him.

She raised her arms, unhurriedly pushing her hair back from her face, hearing his sudden sharp intake of breath as she held the pose for a count of seconds. Then she picked up the dress and slid it over her head. It felt voluptuously cool against her heated skin, curving into her waist and skimming her slender hips as it drifted into place. There was a sweet ache in her breasts as the satin caressed their hardening peaks, and she knew that his own body would be experiencing a similar response.

She slipped her arms into the long sleeves, then paused, almost startled, as she glimpsed herself suddenly in the long wall mirror. She wouldn't have dared choose it for herself, but now she saw how the deep, dramatic colour heightened the flame in her hair and turned her skin to milk. As he'd known it would.

She felt different—exotic—all inhibitions flown.

She turned gracefully and walked towards him, barefoot, holding the unfastened bodice against her, the skirt whispering about her knees.

She said sedately, 'I need help with the zip, please,' and turned her back to him.

She half-heard, half-sensed that he'd got up from the chair. There was a pause and Adrien tensed, scarcely breathing, waiting...

He sighed, burying his face in her hair, then letting his hands slide under the edges of the dress and close softly on her breasts. She leaned back against him, moving her hips slowly, letting her body brush his with deliberate enticement, blind to everything but the urgent demand of her own sensuality.

His hands skimmed her inflamed nipples, drawing a soft whimper from her throat.

He turned her in his arms, his hand tangling in her hair, quenching the fierceness of his kiss in the moist compliance of her parted lips.

When he lifted his head, she could hear the rasp of his breathing, and reached up to draw him down to her again. But he shook his head, his mouth curling into a crooked smile.

He said quietly, 'It would be so easy, Adrien—and so impossible. Because I need more than you have to give. And I won't settle for less.'

He put her from him, gently but decisively, and walked to the door. She clutched the dress against her, her eyes wide with disbelief as she watched him go. At the door, he turned.

He said, 'As I tried to tell you earlier, I have another guest arriving during the weekend.' He paused, then added with cool finality, 'I've told Jean to put her in the room next to mine.'

And went.

It was a long time before she moved. Before she was capable of a simple action like taking off the dress and hanging it up. Before she could make her arms and legs obey her, and force her dazed mind to come to terms with what had just happened to her.

There was a girl looking back at her from the mirror, a stranger, naked except for a tiny triangle of lace, whose face looked haggard in the growing shadows of the room. Someone who looked solitary, and frighteningly vulnerable.

She stared at this girl, trying to view her dispassionately. To see her as Chay would have seen her only a few minutes before—the small, high breasts, the tapering waist and slender legs. Her eyes shadowy with promise. Her semi-nude body in itself an invitation.

But desirable? She could no longer be sure of anything. Least of all her own untried sexuality.

With a tiny cry, Adrien swooped on her robe and huddled it on, and turned away, as if that, somehow, would obliterate the image from her mind.

So much for all the heart-searching she'd subjected herself to, she thought, her throat closing. At the very moment she'd found the courage to tell Chay she'd been wrong about him he'd been trying to tell her that it no longer mattered.

That he'd found someone else with whom he'd share a future instead of a past. Someone who'd value him for the man he'd become rather than the bitter figure of vengeance she'd created in her mind.

He had wanted her, she thought. There had been moments when she'd been quite certain of that. Because he was subject to temptation like everyone else. And tonight had been, briefly, one of those moments.

But in the end he'd walked away, because he was reinventing his life and she no longer had a place in it. Because it was more important to him to keep faith with the new woman he'd found than give way to some transient physical impulse.

It might even have been her disastrous attempt at surrender to him which had made the final decision for him, she thought, her hands clenching in involuntary pain. Which had convinced him that the bargain he'd forced on her was not what he wanted after all, but just a sterile, soulless diversion.

Perhaps it had made him see how much his new lady meant to him, she thought, swallowing. And that was why he'd returned to London with such haste. To give her the commitment and assurances that she deserved. To put the past, and its questions, behind him once and for all.

And now, when it was too late, she knew with startling clarity that it no longer mattered to her what Chay had done, or what he'd been. That it was meaningless to go on doubting him.

Because she was his, and he was hers, for all eternity, and she hungered for him with every breath she drew.

And no amount of time or distance would ever change that. Nor the cold rationality of accepting that he'd chosen someone else and that she was condemned to a wilderness of loneliness.

She gave a small moan and clamped her hands over her mouth to stifle it.

She was like the boy who'd cried 'wolf'. She'd told herself over and over again that it was just a job, that there was no emotion involved and she could walk away unscathed at the end. And now Chay had taken her at her word. The contract was broken. The link severed. And only she knew that she was bleeding to death.

There would come a time when she could grieve for what she had lost, but now she needed every ounce of resolve to get through this weekend. To smile and entertain Chay's business guests. To earn, with charm and efficiency, the money that had saved her from disaster. And to bow out with grace when the new lady of the house arrived. Pride demanded that much.

She might not be needed at all, she thought bleakly. Perhaps, on balance, Chay might prefer her to leave at once, ridding himself of any lingering temptation and an inconvenient reminder of the past in one fell swoop.

She wrapped the robe round her more securely and went out of her room. At the other end of the corridor she could see that the door of the guest room adjoining the master suite was standing open, and as she stood, hesitating, Mrs Whitley appeared from the linen room, carrying towels.

Adrien imitated a smile. 'I hear we're having an extra guest,' she said brightly.

'Oh, Mr Haddon has told you, madam.' The housekeeper appeared relieved. 'I understand it was rather a last-minute decision, and he was concerned that it might put us out.'

'I'm sure we can cope,' Adrien said quietly, following the older woman along the corridor. 'Is there anything I can do to help?'

'No, thanks, madam.' Mrs Whitley beamed at her. 'I'm used to the way she likes things done by now.'

'I see,' was all Adrien could find to say to that. So this was an established relationship after all, she thought. And perhaps there'd been a slight glitch somewhere along the way which had turned Chay's thoughts briefly towards alternative amusement. Only for him to realise the error of his ways...

All the arrangements seemed perfect, she acknowledged

as she stood rigidly in the doorway. It wasn't the largest of the guest rooms but it was one of her favourites, with its pretty chintzes. There were bowls of flowers everywhere, and the bed looked inviting, with pillows piled high and crisp linen.

Not that the lady concerned would be spending much time there, she thought, wincing. Her nights would undoubtedly be passed with Chay in the big canopied bed next door. She would be the one in his arms, responding rapturously to the caress of his hands on her skin, listening as his voice whispered his love for her.

She cleared her throat. 'I've got a bit of a headache, Mrs Whitley. Do you think I could have dinner on a tray in my room?'

'Of course, Miss Lander.' Was there understanding as well as sympathy in the housekeeper's glance? 'Would you prefer a light supper? Can I get you some paracetamol?'

'I have some.' And what painkiller on earth could relieve the agony that was grinding inside her? Adrien wondered as she turned to retreat. 'Something simple would be fine, if it's no trouble.' She hesitated. 'If you'd just tell Mr Haddon that I won't be coming down…'

'Oh, he's dining out himself, madam,' Mrs Whitley said briskly. 'He told me so just now. It's not a problem.'

How desperate we are to avoid each other, Adrien thought, as she trailed back to her room. But perhaps even that's for the best.

And she wished with all her heart that she could believe it.

She spent the evening in her room. Mrs Whitley brought her supper of mushroom soup and a herb omelette, followed by chocolate mousse, and, taking one look at her white strained face, recommended an early night. Then stood over her while Adrien swallowed the painkillers for the fictional headache which had now become full-blown reality.

It seemed impossible that she should sleep, yet she did. When she woke the sun was streaming through the curtains and for a brief moment the day seemed full of promise. Until she remembered.

But it was only the morning she had to get through, she told herself resolutely, getting out of bed. In the afternoon Chay's visitors would be arriving, and she would have no time to spare for her own thoughts.

She had the dining room to herself when she went downstairs, a used cup and plate indicating that Chay had already breakfasted.

She drank some of the fresh coffee that Mrs Whitley brought her, and crumbled a piece of toast to pieces in lieu of eating.

She cleared the table and put the used dishes on a tray to take to the kitchen. The cleaners had arrived, and were already hard at work, she saw, as she emerged from the dining room.

Adrien thought she had never seen the Grange look more beautiful. In spite of everything that had happened since, it had been a privilege to plan its restoration and watch the house slowly revive.

It was a labour of love, she thought, and sighed.

'There's a fax for you.' Chay was standing in the office doorway, holding a sheet of paper. He was wearing close fitting black trousers and a matching polo shirt open at the neck. He looked heavy-eyed, in need of a shave, and not a little bad-tempered, and Adrien's heart turned over in love and longing at the sight of him.

She said coolly, 'Thank you,' as he dropped the paper on to the tray. The message was brief: 'Come over around coffee time. I have a surprise for you. Zelda.'

'You should have explained to her that I have first call on your time this weekend,' Chay said with equal coldness.

'Everything's ready.' Adrien lifted her chin. 'I think I should be allowed half an hour off for good behaviour.' She hesitated. 'In fact, I was wondering whether you really needed me at all.'

His mouth tightened. 'What the hell does that mean?'

She said quietly, 'Your—other guest. Won't she expect to act as your hostess?'

He shook his head. 'She'd hate it. She tends to be shy,' he added wryly.

Her brows lifted. 'So presumably your future entertaining will be kept to a minimum.'

'You can let me worry about that.' His voice and expression were uncompromising. 'And make sure you're back in good time.'

'Yes.' Adrien bit her lip. 'Yes, of course.'

She went to the utility room and loaded the dirty crockery into the dishwasher. Mrs Whitley was there, taking things out of the tumble dryer.

'Our boss isn't in a very good mood today.' Adrien kept her tone deliberately light.

Mrs Whitley pursed her lips. 'Hangover,' she said succinctly.

'Oh,' said Adrien.

Just before eleven, she took the Jeep to the village. Zelda was waiting for her, the coffee already made.

'So, what's the surprise?'

'I decided the little black dress needed some help.' Zelda handed her a flat package. When Adrien opened it, she found a waistcoat in black and silver brocade.

'When on earth did you make this?' She slipped it on over her workaday cream shirt. 'It's gorgeous.'

'I made it last night. It's furnishing fabric—left over from that little sitting room we did for Lady Gilmour.'

Zelda grinned at her. 'The old bag's not coming to dinner, I hope?'

'No, just to the drinks party tomorrow.' Adrien paused. 'But I may not be going to that.'

'Why not?' Zelda stared at her. 'I thought you were signed up for the duration.'

Adrien shrugged. 'Things keep changing.' She took the waistcoat off and folded it carefully. She said in a low voice, 'Zee—I don't think I can take any more.'

'Oh, dear.' Zelda sighed deeply. 'This is what I was afraid of. You've fallen in love.'

Adrien smoothed the brocade with her fingertip. She said simply, 'I've loved him all my life.'

'Adie,' Zelda said gently, 'a few weeks ago you were planning to marry Piers Mendoza.'

Adrien bent her head wretchedly. 'I was fooling myself,' she said. 'I'd never have gone through with it. I was more in love with the house than I ever was with Piers. But he was there—and he was a link with the past and he seemed to want me,' she added with difficulty. 'Besides, I'd convinced myself that Chay would never come back. And that I hated him. I—needed to hate him because of everything that had gone on in the past. So I built up this whole big illusion about being in love with Piers.'

'My God.' Zelda cast her eyes to heaven. 'And then Chay did come back.'

'Yes.' Adrien gave a brief, unhappy smile. 'And now I've lost him.' She paused. 'He—he has someone else.'

Zelda grimaced. 'It's becoming an epidemic. Who is she?'

'I don't know. But he's invited her down this weekend and put her in the room next to his. And I don't think I can stand it,' she ended wretchedly.

Zelda was silent for a moment. 'You're sure it isn't still the house?' Her tone was dry.

Adrien gasped. 'Of course not.' Her voice shook. 'It's always been Chay. Only I was so muddled...' She tried to smile again. 'It was much easier to hate him.'

'Oh, love.' Zelda put her arms round her and gave her a swift hug. 'Well, I think you have two choices. We can sell up here and move far enough away that you'll never see or hear of him again. And they say, "Out of sight, out of mind."'

'Yes,' Adrien agreed listlessly. 'What's the other choice?'

Zelda shrugged. 'If you want him, fight for him.'

'I don't think I have the right weapons.'

'Oh, come on,' Zelda said bracingly. 'He's male; you're female. That usually works pretty well.' She gave Adrien a measuring look. 'After all, that's what this whole thing is about. I never went for that "just a job" story. You've been lit up like a Christmas tree since that first day. And that certainly never happened with Piers.'

Adrien flushed. 'I didn't realise I was that transparent.'

Zelda smiled at her. 'Babe, you've never admitted your true feelings before—even to yourself. It makes a difference. Now, go into battle—and win.'

As Adrien went into the cottage to collect her mail the phone was ringing. She picked up the handset and gave her name and number, but no one answered and then the caller rang off.

Adrien pulled a face at the phone. 'If it's a wrong number you could at least apologise,' she muttered.

She began to go through her letters, tossing junk mail into the wastebasket and putting bills and personal letters to one side.

She was trying to decipher a message on a postcard from Mykonos, from an old schoolfriend, when someone knocked at the front door. Still frowning over her postcard, she wandered over to the door and turned the handle.

'Hello, beauty.' Piers Mendoza smiled at her. 'Surprised to see me?' And, laughing, he pulled her towards him and kissed her.

CHAPTER ELEVEN

For a moment, shock held Adrien still, then she pulled away, furiously scrubbing a hand across her mouth.

'What the hell are you doing here?'

'I was in the area,' he said.

'Was that you on the phone just now?'

'I was checking you were here. After all, I could hardly turn up at the Grange, and I gather that's where you're living these days.' His voice deepened, became almost pleading. 'I had to see you, Adrien. I had to explain. To put things right between us.'

She went on staring at him, her eyes wide with disbelief. 'But you're in Brazil.'

His mouth thinned. 'Don't remind me. But I had some unfinished business in London, so I came back two days ago.'

She said tersely, 'You should have stayed in London. Goodbye, Piers.' She made to close the door, but he slipped past her, shutting it himself and leaning against it.

'You could at least hear me out,' he told her reproachfully.

'There's nothing to hear,' she said coldly. 'You conned me, Piers, and I could have gone bankrupt.'

'I was desperate, Adrien.' His voice was suddenly hoarse. 'You don't understand down in this backwater, but it's a jungle out there. And Chay Haddon's one of the tigers. I had no choice. I had to save my own skin.'

'At the expense of mine.'

'You do what you must in order to survive, Adrien.' He

158

shrugged slightly. 'As you've doubtless discovered by now. I'm sure Chay charged highly for his rescue package.'

She bit her lip. 'I don't know what you're talking about.'

He laughed. 'Don't lie, darling. I can see in your eyes you're no longer the dizzy little innocent I left behind. I just hope he made your initiation enjoyable,' he added softly. 'He's waited long enough for it.'

She said shortly, 'You're disgusting. And I'd like you to leave.'

He threw up his hands in capitulation. 'Sweetheart, I'm sorry. I'm just jealous, I guess. I always have been.'

She shook her head in bewilderment. 'But why?'

'Because my uncle preferred him.' He spoke with sudden harshness. 'A housekeeper's bastard above his own nephew. Can you believe it? He was at the Grange the whole time, and I only came on visits, so there was always a chance he could cut me out with Old Angus. Steal my inheritance.'

Adrien said gravely, 'So—he had to be taught a lesson? Was that it?'

'Can you blame me?' He sounded almost injured. 'I wanted him out of the reckoning. It never occurred to me that your dreamy bird-watching hero would turn himself into the tycoon of the Millennium.'

'And take your inheritance, anyway.' Her voice bit.

'Yes,' he said. 'But I made him pay for it. And I added a premium for you, my sweet.' He looked at her with narrowed eyes. 'You've always been his one weakness. It's made—negotiations easier.'

'Chay has no weaknesses,' she said. 'Not any more. So don't expect any favours.'

'Ah.' He studied her speculatively. 'So what's happened, Adrien? Did you finally run out of hero-worship? Or did you fail to—er come up to his expectations?' He grinned. 'Well, that was always on the cards. You're a lovely girl,

Adrien, but you're not that special. And Chay Haddon can afford to pay for any woman he wants—and a wide range of services.'

She walked to the door and threw it open, her eyes blazing. 'Get out—now.'

'I seem to have touched a nerve,' he said, unperturbed. 'Well, we're not all as fussy—or as rich as the great Mr Haddon. And I plan to visit London on a regular basis from now on. Why don't you move back there and rent a place? Let me show you how much fun bed can be?'

She said steadily, 'Because you sicken me. You're sleaze on legs, Piers, and I can't believe I ever let you anywhere near me. Don't contact me again.'

'Harsh words,' he said with a shrug. 'Let's test your resolve.' And he pulled her into his arms and put his mouth on hers.

Her impulse was to struggle. To kick and fight, and mark his face with her nails. But a warning voice reminded her that anger made him dangerous, that it might be better to stand passively and suffer the pressure of his lips and the worm of his tongue trying to invade her mouth.

It was soon over. He smiled at her, but the look in his eyes was ugly. 'Don't worry, Adrien. You won't be hearing from me again. Who needs a cold bitch like you anyway?'

He walked to the Mercedes parked at the kerb, blew her an insolent kiss, then drove away with a squeal of tyres.

She thought, shuddering, I need to wash my face.

She turned to go back into the cottage and saw Chay standing a few yards away, his face like stone.

As their eyes met, Adrien felt her heart stop beating. She seemed to be frozen to the spot, watching him walk towards her.

He said, too quietly, 'So that was the surprise your friend was talking about?'

'No.' She shook her head violently. 'No, that was something completely different. She'd no more idea that Piers had come back than I did.'

'You sound as if he wasn't a welcome visitor.' His mouth was grim. 'Unfortunately for you, I witnessed the tender farewell.'

'No,' she said. 'You thought you saw it. Like I thought I saw you at the treehouse.'

'You weren't exactly fighting him off.'

She stared at him, reading the condemnation in his voice, the contempt. And felt her own anger kindle in response.

She said slowly, 'How dare you judge me? And what concern is it of yours, anyway? I'm working my notice at the Grange, Chay Haddon, and you have no right to interfere in my private affairs.'

He said harshly, 'Tell me this isn't happening, Adrien. That you're not contemplating any kind of relationship with that piece of scum.'

'And he speaks so well of you,' she said mockingly. 'My life's my own, Chay, and I make my own decisions. I don't need your approval.'

'Are you going to see him again?' His hand closed on her arm urgently. 'Answer me.'

'He's asked me.' She couldn't believe she was saying these things, but some demon drove her on. The hurt inside her lashed out at him. 'He wants me to meet him in London.'

'And you're considering it? God.' He shook his head, his face suddenly haggard. 'You're a fool, Adrien.'

'And you're a hypocrite,' she bit back recklessly. 'Don't forget that you're the one who put me on the market in the first place. You can hardly complain if there are other buyers.'

'I'm not likely to forget.' He was white. 'It's going to haunt me for the rest of my life. But you can't do this, Adrien. You don't know what he's really like.'

'And you're so much better?' she challenged, and shook her head derisively. 'No, Chay. You have your life and I have mine. I'll make my choices, and you won't stop me.'

'Ultimately, perhaps not.' His tone was hard. 'But while you're working for me you won't chase him back to London. My car's down the road. You're coming with me.'

'I have the Jeep…'

'It can stay here. I'm keeping you chained to my wrist this weekend, Adrien. When it's over you're free to ruin your future in any way that seems good to you. Until then, you still belong to me.'

'Oh?' She lifted her head defiantly. 'How do you plan to explain that to your lady guest?'

'She'll understand,' he said. 'Unlike you, Adrien, she trusts me.'

Her laugh rasped her throat. 'And you call *me* a fool.'

'Piers is a married man,' he said. 'I am not.'

'Not yet, perhaps.' The knife inside her twisted slowly, but she didn't falter. 'But you plan to be. Isn't that right?'

'Yes,' he said. 'But, unlike Piers, when I'm married my wife will never have cause to doubt my fidelity. My woman, her man, until death parts us.' He paused. 'Now, let's go home.'

'I am at home.'

He smiled bleakly. 'Of course you are. I phrased that badly. Is there anything you need before we return to the workplace?'

'My bag and some letters.' She went in and scooped them up from the hall table, then turned to find him standing just behind her.

She said between her teeth, 'The world lost a great policeman when you decided to become a property tycoon.'

He said equally, 'Lack of trust works both ways, darling. Now, is there any possibility of declaring a truce—at least until my guests depart? The continual sniping could be a serious embarrassment—and very boring for the audience.'

'Fine,' she said. 'Truce declared. As long as I can go when the guests go.'

'Agreed,' he said wearily. 'I won't try to stop you again.'

She supposed, in its way, it was a small victory. But as she followed Chay to the car it felt far more like a crushing defeat.

Whatever her personal feelings, Adrien had to admit as they drove home from the Country Club on Saturday that the weekend seemed to be going well.

To her surprise, she had found she genuinely liked the three couples whom Chay had invited, although apart from Madame Byron, who was in her thirties, they were all considerably older than she was.

The oldest of the wives was Arlena Travis, a plump, grey-haired, exquisitely groomed American with a Southern drawl like warm honey.

Barbara James lived in London's Holland Park, but confessed to Adrien that her long-term ambition was to persuade her husband to move back to Suffolk, where she'd been born and raised, because she missed the countryside so much.

Nathalie Byron's English was nowhere near as good as her husband's, and she'd tended to say little at dinner the first evening. When they'd adjourned to the drawing room for coffee, Adrien had dragged up her 'A' level French course from the recesses of her memory and had begun to talk to the elegant Parisienne slowly and carefully, in her own language, with the other two eventually joining in with much laughter and pauses for correction in grammar and pronunciation.

Adrien had wondered how the wives would regard her, even though Chay had introduced her formally as his associate. She certainly doubted her ability to play her part adequately. Yet they seemed to accept her without question.

Even the all-purpose black dress had acquired some belated chic with Zelda's waistcoat.

'Why, that's so lovely,' Mrs Travis had said before they'd gone into dinner. 'Where did you get it?'

'My business partner made it for me,' Adrien said, aware that Chay was standing within earshot. 'It was a surprise.'

Another, less welcome surprise was how devastating Chay looked in formal evening clothes. It was the first time Adrien had ever seen him in a dinner jacket, and she was stunned, her heart beating painfully, her stomach lurching whenever he came into her line of vision.

She was seriously glad when the evening drew to an end, and no one wanted to stay up to the small hours. The day had been a strained one, and she was tired. She was wearing her hair up in a loose knot, and she'd just unfastened it and shaken it loose when she heard a tap at her door.

When she opened it, Chay was standing there. He'd unfastened the top buttons of his shirt, and his black tie was dangling from his fingers.

He said gravely, 'I wanted to thank you for the effort you put in with Nathalie Byron. Henri was very impressed. He worries that she sometimes feels isolated on this sort of occasion.' His smile did not reach his eyes. 'I'm—grateful.'

'It was my pleasure,' Adrien said. 'She's charming.'

'You did well,' he said. 'And you looked very beautiful, very relaxed.' He brushed the shoulder of the waistcoat with the tip of his fingers. 'I like the surprise,' he added. 'Goodnight.'

Her lips framed her own goodnight, but it was a soundless whisper that followed him as he walked away. All evening he'd shown her the same polite friendliness, and it terrified her.

Because it showed her the bleakness of a future where

she would never know what it was to be truly a woman. Because it was Chay, and Chay alone, who could awaken her body's responses. And without him she was condemned to physical and emotional sterility.

She wanted to run after him and throw herself into his arms. She wanted to plead with him to take her and make her complete. To join his nakedness to hers and compel her surrender.

But she didn't dare to do any of those things, because another rejection could destroy her.

Zelda had told her to fight for him, she remembered as she turned slowly away and shut her door. Instead, because of Piers, she'd ended up fighting with him. And now they were strangers, facing each other across some endless abyss.

And today she'd hardly seen him, she thought now, because all the men had gone to play golf. At the Country Club she'd played tennis with Nathalie, and two other women whom the professional had introduced to them. They'd all had a swim in the pool, and a massage, and visited the beauty treatment rooms.

'My stars, but I'm looking forward to my dinner,' Arlena Travis said happily as the car turned into the Grange's drive. 'There's nothing like a day's pampering to give you a healthy appetite.'

Adrien agreed, but her own stomach was suddenly churning nervously. She'd caught sight of a strange car—a red Peugeot—standing outside the house. The other guest had arrived at last, she realised, swallowing.

Perhaps the new formality between Chay and herself might help her get through the next difficult few hours, she told herself, without much hope.

'She's in her room, Miss Lander,' Mrs Whitley returned when Adrien asked, with a certain constraint, where the newcomer was. 'She's had a trying journey, and she's resting.'

Not only shy, but fragile too, Adrien thought wryly, as she went up to change for the drinks party. Was that really what Chay wanted?

She showered, dried her hair, and pinned it into a topknot again. She applied cosmetics with more than usual care, blotting out the violet shadows under her eyes and smoothing blusher delicately on to her cheekbones. She needed a public face to hide behind tonight.

She hesitated for a long time in front of the wardrobe, then chose a slim-fitting black skirt and a white silk blouse. She had just finished buttoning the blouse when there was a peremptory rap at her door and Chay's voice called, 'Adrien—are you ready yet? People will be arriving soon.'

'Almost there,' she returned, slipping her feet into high-heeled black pumps. 'I'll be down in two minutes.'

She'd expected him to leave it at that, but when she opened her door he was still standing there, his frowning gaze sweeping her.

He said abruptly, 'I asked you to wear the dress I brought you.'

'I'd—rather not.' Her voice sounded stifled.

His voice gentled. 'Adrien—it's your last evening in my employ. Indulge me—please.' His mouth twisted. 'You can always look on it as a uniform.'

She looked past him rigidly. 'Just as you wish,' she said at last, and turned back into the room.

'I'll wait,' he said. 'In case you need help with the zip.'

She shook her head as she closed the door. 'I can manage—really.'

The silken dress slid over her head, clinging to her slender curves as if it loved her. Closing the zip was a struggle, but she persevered, knowing unhappily that she dared not risk even the most fleeting intimate contact with Chay.

She turned slowly in front of the mirror, watching the subtle flare of the skirt and the play of the dark crimson sheen that altered her every movement. It was beautiful, she thought, and probably the most sophisticated dress she'd ever worn.

At least, she thought, I'll be bowing out in style. And, sighing, she went downstairs to join the others.

As she hesitated in the drawing room doorway they all turned to look at her, and the involuntary murmur of appreciation brought real colour to her face. Only Chay was silent, his face coolly expressionless as he studied her.

'Honey, you look like a million dollars,' said Mrs Travis, herself resplendent in a silk knit suit in shades of mother of pearl. 'That colour's like something from an old painting.'

'It's called Venetian red.' Adrien came forward, recovering some of her composure now that a lightning glance round the room had revealed only familiar faces.

'Ah, Venice.' The older woman sighed pleasurably. 'One of my all-time favourite cities.' She gave Adrien a slight conspiratorial nudge. 'And heaven for a honeymoon.'

Adrien, burningly aware of Chay's cynical glance, murmured something indistinguishable and escaped to talk to Nathalie Byron instead.

She was standing with her back to the door when she heard Chay's voice, warm with affection, saying, 'So there you are at last, darling. Come and be introduced to everyone.'

For a moment Adrien felt herself freeze, then she mustered a too-bright smile and braced herself to turn and look at the woman framed in the doorway. And halted, her eyes widening incredulously.

The newcomer was tall and slim, dressed elegantly in black. Her silver hair was cut in a sleek bob, and there were pearls at her throat and in her ears.

She said in a quiet, clear voice, 'Not everyone, Chay. I see one old friend, at least.' She walked across the room and took Adrien's nerveless hand in hers. 'How are you, Adrien?'

Adrien said numbly, 'Mrs Haddon? But I don't understand...'

'I'm actually Mrs Stretton now.' Grey eyes just like her son's surveyed her calmly. There was a sadness in their depths, and a network of fine lines on her skin. 'Angus and I were married just after he went to Spain.'

Adrien shook her head, feeling winded. 'I had no idea.' She turned accusingly to Chay. 'You didn't tell me.'

His voice was cool. 'You never asked.'

It was true, Adrien realised to her shame. She'd not even enquired whether his mother was still alive, let alone what had happened to her.

Oh, God, she whispered silently. How could I be so thoughtless—so unthinking?

She said quietly, 'I'm so sorry. It's good to see you again, Mrs Stretton.'

'Do we have to be so formal? I'd much prefer you to call me Margaret.' Her glance appraised Adrien again, and she nodded at Chay. 'You were right about the dress, darling. It's quite perfect for her.' She patted her arm. 'Now, please introduce me to your other guests.'

How many shocks could you absorb in one day before you fell to pieces? Adrien wondered as she dazedly complied.

It was better when other people started arriving and she was fully occupied in making sure everyone had a drink and someone to talk to, ensuring the trays of nibbles were being circulated. Because it gave her no time to think, or weigh up the implications of it all. Or contemplate all the unanswered questions. The time for that was still to come.

She stayed on the move, carefully maintaining the length of the room between Chay and herself.

'Such a lovely party,' she heard on all sides. 'You must come to us for dinner—for drinks—for bridge...' And she smiled and said something grateful and noncommittal, allowing them to think she would still be around to accept those obligations.

'What a wonderful surprise.' Lady Gilmour cornered her. 'I knew Angus Stretton's first wife had died, poor thing, but I had no idea he'd married again.'

'I really don't know anything about the background to it all, Lady Gilmour...'

Lady Gilmour lowered her voice discreetly. 'She was a complete invalid. She lost a baby quite early in the marriage and had a terrible nervous breakdown. She spent several years in a nursing home, and just as she seemed to be better they realised she'd contracted one of those terrible wasting diseases with an impossible name.

'Angus was quite heartbroken, of course. He used to visit her faithfully, and made sure she had the best of care and all the latest treatment.'

She sighed faintly. 'No one blamed him for finding happiness with Margaret, and they were both very circumspect. She pretended to be a widow with a child, and we pretended to believe it. It would have been terrible if Ruth had heard so much as a whisper, but I don't believe she ever did.'

Adrien stared at her. She was remembering Chay, seated at Angus's desk, and the feeling that she was seeing a ghost.

She said, stumbling a little, 'Chay is Angus Stretton's son? Is that what you're saying?'

'Yes, of course, my dear.' Lady Gilmour's face was astonished. 'I thought you of all people would have known.

Your father and Angus were such friends—and you—well, you were almost part of the family.'

She gave Adrien a warm smile. 'And we're all delighted to know that you're at the Grange again. How well everything's turned out, after all. Now, I must have a quick word with Mrs Grimes about the Garden Club. I don't believe the new treasurer will do at all...' And she disappeared purposefully.

Adrien stood clutching her untouched glass, her mind spinning as she tried to assimilate what she'd just been told. Chay was Angus's son, she thought, yet he'd been sent away twice in disgrace and Angus had allowed it to happen. Allowed Piers to remain as his official heir. But why?

Chay said softly, 'People are beginning to leave.'

Her own voice was urgent. 'Chay, I need to talk to you. I've only just realised about you—and Angus...'

'Well?' he said. 'What about it?'

She stared up at him. 'How can you ask? It—it changes everything.'

'No,' he said, quite gently. 'It doesn't change a thing. And I think everything necessary's been said already. Now, help me say goodbye.'

She went with him mutely, wincing from the hurt of his dismissive words. It occurred to her that the door into his life had just been finally closed against her. That she was now doomed to stay outside, cold and alone, for the rest of her days.

And the realisation filled her with terror.

CHAPTER TWELVE

THE success of the drinks party carried over into dinner. Mrs Whitley had excelled herself. An exquisite seafood salad was followed by baby chickens cooked with white wine and grapes, and an amaretto soufflé. Margaret Stretton's arrival had provided a new focus for attention, and, far from seeming shy, she was coping with great charm and aplomb.

The laughter and talk gave Adrien a perfect opportunity to be quiet with her bewildered and unhappy thoughts. It was as if all these years she'd been staring into a distorting mirror. And now for the first time she was free to see things as they really were.

And realise, too, what a culpable fool she'd been, she lashed at herself.

There was sudden quiet round the table, and Adrien looked up with a start to see Chay push back his chair and rise to his feet.

He said, 'I'd like to propose a toast to Adrien—who took a neglected house and turned it back into a home. She's been working as my assistant to make sure everything was ready to welcome you all this weekend, and now it's time for her to move on—return to her own life—her own career.'

He lifted his glass. 'Success and happiness, Adrien.'

As the words echoed round the table, and they drank to her, Adrien saw Arlena Travis's brows lift, and the other women exchanging surprised looks with their husbands. She bent her head, her skin warming with faint colour. She had not expected such a public dismissal.

'There's one more thing.' Chay reached into an inside pocket in his dinner jacket and extracted a slim flat box. He walked round the table to Adrien's side.

'I have a farewell present for you,' he said. 'A keepsake to remind you of all the time we've spent together.' He put the box on the table in front of her. His face was still, his eyes unreadable.

Her fingers shook as she removed the lid, because she knew what she was going to see and she didn't know how to deal with it. She made a small choked sound as the dark red stones of the garnet pendant gleamed up at her, and Chay lifted it from its white satin bed and fastened its slender golden chain round her neck.

'The original clasp was faulty,' he said. 'But I've had it fixed.'

She had almost forgotten how beautiful it was. How the stones seemed to possess their own inner flame. She looked down, watching them shimmer against her pale skin, and touched them with one finger delicately, fearfully, as if they might burn.

'Thank you.' Her voice was a stranger's. 'I never expected—anything like this.'

She looked up at him, searching his cool, enigmatic face, begging silently for enlightenment. But he turned away and went back to his seat.

'My stars.' Arlena Travis leaned forward. 'That is one glorious piece of jewellery, honey.' She gave it the shrewd look of a connoisseur, then nodded. 'And very old, as well as valuable. Does it have a history?'

'Oh, yes.' It was Margaret Stretton who spoke, her tone reflective. 'Originally it was bought by a young man as a birthday gift for the girl he wanted to marry. But his parents, rightly or wrongly, felt she was too young to make such a serious commitment, and that any mention of marriage might even scare her away.'

Adrien realised she had almost stopped breathing. She found herself staring at the older woman as if she was mesmerised.

'There were other obstacles, too,' Margaret Stretton went on. 'Quite serious ones. So it was agreed it would be safer to offer the pendant as simply a family gift, without strings, and that the young man should start to woo her gently and without pressure.'

She sighed. 'But unfortunately it all went wrong, and instead they parted in great bitterness.'

She smiled round the table. 'Not a very happy story, but all in the past. It certainly doesn't matter any more. And I'm glad the pendant's found a good home at last.'

And what about me? Adrien wanted to shout aloud, her hands gripping each other in her lap until her fingers ached. Don't I matter any more either?

Well, she had the answer to that round her throat. The pendant was a farewell gift. What was sometimes known as a 'kiss-off'—except that there hadn't been that many kisses...

As a mistress, she'd hardly even registered, she acknowledged with a wry twist of her heart.

She stared across at Chay, willing him to look at her, but he was talking to Nathalie Byron and she could only see his profile, strong but oddly remote.

Unreachable, she thought as pain wrenched at her.

She pushed back her chair and rose, a smile pinned on. 'Ladies, I think our coffee will be in the drawing room by now. Shall we go?'

It was not an easy interlude. No one asked Adrien directly why she was leaving, but she could feel curiosity simmering around her and she poured the coffee and handed the cups, and smiled and chatted as if she didn't have a care in the world.

Barbara James came and sat with her, talking generally and gently about the restoration of the house, and the problems it had thrown up, then asking for advice on the redecoration of a rather cold north-facing bathroom in her London home.

Adrien responded gratefully, thankful for a question she could actually answer.

When Barbara moved on, her place was taken by Arlena Travis.

'I've come for a closer look at that necklace,' she announced, putting on her glasses. 'Antique jewellery is my passion, so I guess my husband is real glad someone beat him to this piece.'

She gave a deep sigh of appreciation. 'That is some love-token, honey. Now, I'd have done the conventional thing and picked emeralds to go with your hair. But these rubies are just so right for you, somehow. And with that dress—magnificent.'

Adrien put down her coffee cup very carefully on the table in front of her.

She said politely, 'I'm sorry, Mrs Travis. I don't quite understand. These are garnets.'

Mrs Travis gave her an old-fashioned look. 'Oh, come on, honey, are you crazy? These are rubies, and particularly fine ones, too.' She patted Adrien's hand. 'But if you won't take my word for it just get them appraised for insurance. You'll find out.'

Adrien's lips felt numb. She managed, 'I'll be sure and do that.' She gave her companion a meaningless smile and got to her feet. 'Would you excuse me, please?'

She walked across the room to Margaret Stretton. She said, 'Would you take over for me, Mrs Stretton? I—I have a splitting headache and I'd like to go to my room.'

She didn't wait for the reply, just murmuring a general goodnight before she fled.

Safety upstairs, she shut her door behind her and leaned against it, gasping for breath.

Rubies, she thought, her mind reeling. When she was eighteen, Chay had bought her rubies. But hadn't told her. Had let her think the pendant was just a semi-precious trinket.

He couldn't steal his own gift, so why had the pendant vanished, to resurface in his room?

It was Piers, she thought, her throat tightening. How couldn't she have seen it before? Piers, who would also have known the real value of the pendant. And Piers, because it had ostensibly come from Angus Stretton, would have regarded it as part of his inheritance. And resented it being given away.

He'd clearly had no idea that Chay was his cousin. He'd been and always would be 'the housekeeper's bastard'.

But stealing the pendant and planting it in Chay's room must have seemed an ideal way of ridding himself permanently of a hated rival. Because of the value of the stones, Chay would be bound to be arrested. That was how Piers would have reasoned.

And, as a bonus, it would drive a permanent wedge between Chay and the girl he loved. Destroy the new understanding that had arisen since his previous attempt to separate them.

And it hadn't been because Piers had ever wanted her for herself, she realised. Right to the end she'd simply been someone he could use. Even when he'd arrived at the cottage the previous day he'd been able to turn it to his advantage.

And I fell for it, she acknowledged miserably. But why, when everyone knew the truth about the pendant, was he allowed to get away with it? It makes no sense.

Why hadn't Angus Stretton challenged him and thrown

him out? And why had Chay been sent away when he was
guiltless?

She began to walk up and down the room, her arms
wrapped tightly round her body.

She remembered the snatches of conversation between
her parents, the harsh, damaging comments that she'd assumed alluded to Chay. But it had been Piers they'd been
talking about. Piers who had always been demanding
money. Piers who was dangerous.

She thought desolately, How could I have been so
wrong—so blind?

There was still so much she didn't know. And now she
probably never would discover the whole tangled truth.

She undressed and put on her robe, but she didn't get
into bed. She felt too wretched and too restless, and sleep
was a million miles away. Instead she curled up on the
window seat and stared out into the darkness, unhappy
thoughts chasing themselves round in her head.

Eventually she heard the sound of voices as the rest of
the party came upstairs to bed. And then, shortly afterwards, there was a quiet tap at the door.

'Adrien?' It was Margaret Stretton's voice. 'Are you all
right? May I come in?'

For a moment Adrien was sorely tempted to stay quiet,
and pretend she was asleep. Then she realised that the light
from her lamp would be visible under the door, so she
padded across and turned the handle.

'We were concerned about you.' Mrs Stretton walked
into the room. 'I wondered if you'd like some hot chocolate.'

Adrien said stiltedly, 'That's—kind of you. But, no,
thanks.'

The grey eyes surveyed her keenly. 'Poor child,' she said
gently. 'You've had so many shocks this weekend. I'm not
surprised you had to run away.'

'I can't believe I didn't guess.' Adrien's tone was hushed, as if she was talking to herself. 'That I couldn't see Angus and Chay were father and son—when I thought I knew them both so well.'

'You weren't the only one,' Mrs Stretton comforted her. 'And you weren't meant to know—not then. In fact, it was vitally important that no one did.'

'Especially—Piers Mendoza?'

'Yes,' Mrs Stretton said heavily. 'Him above all.'

'But why?'

'Come and sit with me.' Margaret Stretton took Adrien's unwilling hand and led her back to the window seat.

'You never knew Angus's sister Helen,' she began. 'But she was the loveliest girl, and only eighteen when she met Luiz Mendoza, Piers's father, and married him in spite of all Angus could do. He disliked him instinctively, you see, and distrusted him too. He felt that under all the good looks and charm there was genuine evil. Something he'd rarely encountered before.

'He made enquiries through some high-powered connections of his and discovered that Luiz was a minor racketeer, with a finger in all kinds of unsavoury pies in Brazil, and a heavy gambler, too, who lost more often than he won.

'When Piers was still a baby, Helen died—killed in a road accident, apparently by a hit-and-run driver. Her life had been heavily insured the year before by her husband.'

Adrien's hand went to her mouth. 'Oh, God—you mean…?'

Mrs Stretton nodded. 'There was never any proof, but Angus knew that Luiz had arranged it. He'd already got through Helen's own money, and was badly in debt to some very nasty people.' She grimaced. 'Like father, like son.'

She was silent for a moment. 'Luiz knew that Angus's wife was in a private hospital, and would never give him another child, and that Piers was his sole male heir. Angus was convinced he would allow nothing and no one to stand in Piers's way, and he couldn't risk any further threat to his family. So Chay, for his own safety, had to be—the housekeeper's son.

'When Luiz died, Angus was prepared to give Piers a chance, for Helen's sake, but he soon discovered his mistake.' She shook her head. 'Piers might lack his father's complete ruthlessness, but he's adept at dirty tricks—and blackmail. He didn't guess the truth, but he recognised the affection between the two of them and set out to destroy it. Anyone that Angus loved was seen as a threat to his prospects. That's why he pretended to send both of us away and moved to Spain. To let Piers think he'd won.'

'You mentioned—blackmail...?'

Margaret Stretton nodded. 'Piers guessed about us—Angus and I—and threatened to tell his wife. Ruth was so ill—not just physically, but mentally too. She used to have terrible fits of hysteria and depression, even attempting suicide at one point. Angus paid to protect her. To keep her illusions intact. Because she'd become convinced, you see, that one day there'd be a miracle cure and she'd come back—to her home and her marriage.'

There were sudden tears in her eyes. 'She had to be allowed to go on believing that for the short time she had left.'

'Yes,' Adrien said slowly. 'But—it must have been very hard on Chay—as well as you.'

Margaret Stretton smiled. 'Chay is a realist, like me. And he was always determined to carve out his own path to success. He knew, as well, that Piers would never keep the Grange. That he only had to be patient.'

Adrien bit her lip. 'Yes,' she said. 'He's been very—patient.'

Mrs Stretton rose. 'Try and sleep now.' Her voice was kind. 'And don't worry about getting up tomorrow. I'm taking Arlena and the others to the antiques fair. You don't have to do that.'

'Does that mean I'm free to leave?' Adrien asked woodenly.

At the door, Margaret Stretton turned and smiled at her again. 'Of course,' she said. 'If that's what you really want. And only you know that, Adrien. It's your decision entirely. Goodnight, my dear, and sleep well.'

After she'd gone, Adrien sat where she was for a long time.

Then she went to the chest of drawers in the bedroom and found the empty velvet case that had housed the pendant originally. All these years it had reminded her of heartbreak and betrayal. Now it was time to set the record straight.

And to fight.

She arranged the pendant meticulously on its satin bed, then let herself quietly out into the corridor and went to Chay's room.

She didn't knock. Just turned the handle and walked in.

He was standing by the window, staring out. He'd discarded his dinner jacket and black tie, but apart from that he was still fully dressed.

He turned slowly and surveyed her, his face cool, his mouth set. 'Isn't it rather late for social calls?'

'This is the last one, I promise. I won't trouble you again. I came to give you this.' She held the velvet case out to him. 'I can't take it, Chay.' Her voice trembled a little. 'It's cost too much—in all sorts of ways.'

'My God,' he said. 'Have you kept that box all this time? Why, Adrien? To remind yourself how much you hated me?'

She winced. 'Something like that. But it isn't necessary any longer. So, I'm giving it back, along with the rubies.'

'Consider them a productivity bonus.' He made no attempt to take it from her. His eyes were hard. 'Most people expect some kind of golden handshake at the end of a contract.'

'Well, I'm not most people.' She glared at him. 'And I'm not playing your damned games any longer.'

'Games?' he came back at her savagely. 'Who the hell are you to talk to me about playing games?' He shook his head. 'I really thought you were over Piers—that you'd seen through him at last. But, oh, no. At the first opportunity you're back in his arms.

'Well, go to him, Adrien, if he's want you want. But keep the pendant and lock it up in a bank somewhere. You'll need it when he dumps you again. Or when you have to buy him off.'

His laugh was brief and humourless. 'In ancient times they said rubies were an antidote to poison and a cure for grief. I hope that's true, for your sake. Because you're going to need both of them.'

This was the moment for every scrap of courage she'd ever possessed.

She said, 'I've only ever needed you, Chay. Only ever wanted you.'

His mouth tightened. 'That's not true, and we both know it. You were planning to marry him, for God's sake.'

'I'm not proud of that,' she said. 'I never looked past the charm. Perhaps I didn't want to. I was so alone, Chay. So lonely. In my heart, I was waiting and waiting for you to come back. But you never did. And he was a familiar face. Someone from the time before that loneliness.'

'Was it loneliness that sent you back into his arms yesterday?' His voice was harsh. 'I was there, Adrien. I saw you kissing him.'

'No,' she said. 'You saw him kissing me. That's a different thing entirely. And I believe you were meant to see it. Why else were you there?'

He said slowly, 'There was a phone message. Jean took it.' His brows drew together. 'It said you'd met an old friend and wouldn't be back until late.'

'He called me on his mobile at the cottage to make sure I was there. He must have rung the Grange next.' She shook her head. 'He set the trap, and once again we walked into it.'

'You told me that he wanted you back. You admitted it.' Chay's face was still stony.

'You accused me of meeting him behind your back. I was hurt. I hit back.' She spread her hands. 'I have red hair, Chay. That's something that will never change. Or not until I'm old and grey, anyway.'

'You'll never be that, Adrien,' he said quietly. 'The image I'll always have of you is how you looked tonight—in Venetian red with my rubies round your neck.'

'Chay.' Her voice broke on his name. 'Don't…'

'You were a solitary child,' he went on, as if she hadn't spoken. 'I was isolated too. I told myself I preferred it that way. Yet when you weren't there, I always felt—incomplete. All the time you were growing up I had to accept that we'd become strangers. That I had to stand back—stay aloof.'

There was sadness in his eyes, an odd vulnerability twisting his mouth. 'It was a nightmare—waiting for you to stop hating me. Longing for the moment when you'd look at me and smile again. When it finally happened, I felt reprieved—reborn.'

He sighed. 'I'd just started to make some serious money when I saw the pendant. I knew I had to have it for you. I wanted it to be a talisman, to keep you safe until you were ready to marry me. I was going to ask you that weekend. Tell you I'd wait until you were ready.

'None of us had the least idea that Piers would be arriving for your birthday. He just—turned up. I thought you must have invited him.'

'No,' she said vehemently. 'No—never.'

'So I had to change my plan. I couldn't risk him knowing how I felt about you. How serious it was. Because I knew he'd try to destroy it, or take you from me.

'When he stole the pendant and planted it in my room I knew that Angus was right, that he was capable of anything. That next time it could be drugs.

'I couldn't involve you. You were too young—too vulnerable. I told myself it wasn't our time. That one day I'd return and claim you.

'But when I found you again, you were engaged to him.' His voice was suddenly husky. 'Can you imagine how that made me feel? I could see nothing—think of nothing—except you in his arms—his mouth—his hands—touching you—possessing you.'

He shuddered. 'I went slightly crazy. I told myself that you'd belonged to him, but now you'd belong to me, in every way. I planned how I'd take you to bed—how I'd make love to you so completely that he'd be driven from your mind for ever. That you'd forget he ever existed. Until you could see, taste and breathe nothing but me.

'But instead, by forcing myself on you, I ruined everything for both of us. And I can't forgive myself for that.'

'Is that why you wouldn't make love to me again?' Her eyes widened. 'Out of some conviction that you'd hurt me the first time?'

He said tiredly, 'Adie—you were a virgin. I should have known that and treated you differently—with more consideration.'

Her voice was passionate, 'Chay, my darling fool, I didn't want to be considered. I wanted to be loved. I needed you to kiss the hurt away and show me how it ought to be between us. I thought that I'd disappointed you. That you didn't want me any more.'

'I've wanted you all my life.' There was yearning in his voice, and something deeper, too. Something almost primitive, making Adrien's body stir with sudden excitement. 'Throughout all the anger and the hurt and the partings you were the lodestar of my life. You drew me to you always.' His voice roughened. 'I wanted only to keep you safe, and instead I've driven you away.'

She shook her head, untying the sash of her robe. 'Your mother said the choice was mine,' she told him huskily. 'And I choose to stay. Oh, my love, let's stop punishing each other and be happy. I'm yours—if you want me.'

He was shaking as he lifted her into his arms, his mouth burning against her naked skin. The little velvet case fell unnoticed to the floor as he carried her to the bed and followed her down on to it, his hands tearing at his own clothing with savage energy.

Adrien twined her arms round him—her legs. She cried out in shocked pleasure as his mouth tugged at her nipple. His hands grazed her thighs with trembling urgency and she opened herself to him, arching against him voluptuously, her fingertips seeking him, guiding him.

She moaned as he filled her, the sound hoarse, almost pagan. There was no time for niceties or even lover-words. Their mutual need was too fierce, too consuming. The desire to take and be taken too strong. The time for denial— even for gentleness—was over.

She moved with him, her grace against his power, caught, possessed, by this new and overwhelming rhythm. With each thrust she seemed to draw him deeper and deeper inside her, her body clasping him like dark petals round a stem. She felt herself carried closer and closer to the edge of some whirlpool of emotion, and fear mingled with excitement.

Then, far in the depths of her being, she felt the first tiny pulsations of pleasure, like the flutterings of a wild bird. Sensed them building quietly into sweet ripples of delight that suffused her entire being.

And told her there was more.

Sighing, she lifted herself to him in a demand she barely understood, and heard her falling breath change to a whimper as all control was suddenly ripped away by some blind, atavistic force. She was total animal, drinking savagely from his mouth, her hands raking at him, her voice blurred, unrecognisable, urging him on.

Her body convulsed in sweet agony as she was lost, torn apart, dazed and dazzled by the shattering rapture of her climax.

As he came, he gasped for her, his voice hoarse and breathless, as if he was drowning. And she felt the ultimate scalding heat of his possession.

Some time later, he said, 'Are we still alive?'

'Never more so.' She caressed his lips with hers, her hands stroking his sweat-slicked hair. 'How could you know—so completely—what I wanted?'

'Because you're the other half of me.' He kissed her deeply, his tongue teasing and sensual. 'How could I not know?' He paused. 'Marry me, Adie, my one true love. I can't live without you.'

'And you were sending me away.' She put her palms against his chest, savouring the race of his heart.

'But only so that I could follow. You wouldn't have got far. I was hoping that if I let you go—you might miss me and want to come back.' His smile twisted her heart. 'If all else failed, I thought you might want the house.'

'The house is beautiful.' She put her lips to the pulse in his throat. 'But I'd walk out of it tomorrow to go with you.'

'I think we'll stay. It's time there was happiness here—and new life,' he added softly.

'Yes,' she said. 'Ah, yes.' Then, 'We'll build another treehouse.'

'As many as you want.'

'We'll fight,' she warned.

'How else would we make up?' Chay settled her against the pillows and drew the covers over her.

'Does it have to be marriage?' She curved herself into his arms, smiling wickedly. 'I've just begun to enjoy being your mistress.'

His lips touched her hair. 'Nothing need change. Wife by day,' he whispered, 'mistress by night. That's the deal, my love. And there's no negotiation. This time it's for ever.'

'For ever,' she echoed drowsily, and turned, in tenderness and trust, to sleep at last in her lover's arms.

The world's bestselling romance series.

HARLEQUIN®
Presents~

Seduction and Passion Guaranteed!

Your dream ticket to the vacation of a lifetime!

Why not relax and allow Harlequin Presents® to whisk you away
to stunning international locations with our new miniseries…

*Where irresistible men and sophisticated women
surrender to seduction under the golden sun.*

Don't miss this opportunity to
experience glamorous lifestyles
and exotic settings in:

**Robyn Donald's
THE TEMPTRESS OF TARIKA BAY
on sale July, #2336**

**THE FRENCH COUNT'S MISTRESS
by Susan Stephens
on sale August, #2342**

**THE SPANIARD'S WOMAN
by Diana Hamilton
on sale September, #2346**

**THE ITALIAN MARRIAGE
by Kathryn Ross
on sale October, #2353**

FOREIGN AFFAIRS… A world full of passion!

**Pick up a Harlequin Presents® novel and you will enter a world
of spine-tingling passion and provocative, tantalizing romance!**

Available wherever Harlequin books are sold.

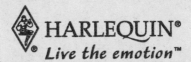

HARLEQUIN®
Live the emotion™

Visit us at www.eHarlequin.com

HPFAMA

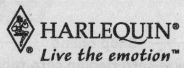

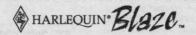

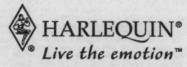